War, Love, and the Absolute

Albert Oon

SHORT STORIES WITH EXTRAS

A True Heart's Test

Chapter 1 – Finding Your True Heart

Today's another day and it's another day I don't feel like living. Not because I have any kind of depression or because I feel physically ill. Instead, I feel mentally ill because of the repetition of my everyday life. It's all fruitless community work. Help out so and so with their animals on the farm, help garden, help clean someone's house, take care of the neighbor's children, clean the floors of the church, and so on and so on. As far as I'm concerned, I'm a slave to my town.

"Oh, you'll get used to it," another community service member says.

"The people appreciate what you do," I'll hear said to me.

"It's not easy, but it's good honest work."

Yada-yada-yada. The only time I felt appreciated for my work was when a random boy five years younger than me made a purple, red, and blue bracelet for me for helping him clean his house. It's the one time I got anything extra for working and felt appreciated for my work because of his kind and appreciative words and want to know more about what I do, so it feels like an irreplaceable treasure to me and I wear it every day. It's a shame that I don't always see him since he's at school, but I do try to see him when I'm not working, which is rare. My parents say I need to work as much as possible to be noticed and get a real job that has better pay and more honor in performing it. I do as they say, not because I want to do as they say, but because I want to live on my own as soon as I can though, at this rate, I'll be an old lady just like the other girls that worked this kind of job. Actually, I might not even get out of this job since many old people still work it because they either love it or because they'll be poor without it. Even if they get promoted and get to work for kings, queens, the Church, and the like, they'll have to work till they're old and have to have someone take care of them.

"Are you daydreaming again, Cornelia?" my mother asks me.

"Yes, I am. It's not like I need to go to work yet," I say while continuing to sit on the porch and look out into the forest and then up at the sky.

My mother says something to me, but I don't listen. Instead, I just try to enjoy looking into the sky and in the forest as much as possible. I don't even know why I waste my time doing this because it's a small joy that makes me want to go back to it during work. It's like the few times my parents and I go on vacation. The relaxation just makes me want it more and hate being at work even more.

While my mother is still talking to me, my father comes out presumably to say something else. He looks like he's about to say something until he is stopped by a portal appearing in front of the house, which I ignore and continue to look up at the sky because I know who's coming out of it.

"Cornelia! How's it going?" the guy coming out of the portal says before the portal behind him closes.

"Eh," I say.

"Cornelia! Get up and greet your best friend. I'm sorry, Eleazar. She's in a bit of a mood today like usual," my mother says.

Ha! Best friend. He's nothing like that. You're always in a mood too, mother, but you always deny it.

"It's okay. I can understand Cornelia's annoyed language. She's glad to see me as I am to see her," Eleazar says.

I think it's better to say that he's lying and he knows he is. Eleazar sits next to me to look up at the sky before looking at me. Now, whatever good feelings I got from looking up at the sky are ruined, so I stand up. Getting a better look at him, I feel so underdressed compared to him. His long black hair is in a ponytail and he wears a gold outfit with black and red trims and a heart necklace around his neck. This along with his black boots was given to him by the Church and the royalty that he serves as a sign of their thanks and his work. In comparison, my grey dress with light gold lines around my neck, sleeves, and waist and my grey boots make me look like I'm homeless.

"What are you doing here?" I ask.

"I don't know. I'm still trying to figure that out. You know how my portals work now," he says.

"It was better when your heart wasn't completely dedicated to the Absolute. You could go anywhere you already were."

"Hey, don't say that. Thanks to my dedication, I can create portals to go anywhere and the Absolute brings me to where I need to go. When our hearts are completely dedicated to the Absolute, we are completely ourselves and can do what we were created to do."

"Oh yeah? Then why don't I have an ability like yours? I've done my fair share of praying and trying to be the best person I can and I've got nothing to show for it."

"But you do! You help our hometown in so many ways. You're so unbelievably talented."

"I'm so unbelievably replaceable. There are tons of people who do the same kind of job that I do and many of them do it better."

"I'm glad you said it," my father as comes out of the house all dressed up.

"Don't you have to go to work?" I say to him.

"I am. Love you and see you later."

"Sure."

"He's just joking, Cornelia. Your father and mother really do love you."

"Whatever. Look, I can't make portals, pull swords out of nothing, breathe fire, summon animals, none of the special abilities that I hear a lot about and even see in this town. I'll be just like my parents and their parents before them by being stuck working this thankless poor job for the rest of my life."

"I didn't get the ability to teleport anywhere until I was a teenager and my parents are hard workers just like yours with no magical abilities. Having parents with normal abilities doesn't mean that you'll have the same ones for your whole life. Don't you remember the stories?"

"I know about them, but those abilities typically change around our age. There hasn't been any kind of change in me."

This is one of the reasons why my parents like Eleazar more than me. They always talk about him as if he's some kind of hero I should follow in his example. He had a luxurious life handed to him by royalty when word of his heart's ability reached them. Now, he's an escort for all kinds of kings, queens, and high ranking clergy members. He's talking to me about the Absolute and how I should appreciate what I have, but I ignore it because I hate these speeches he gives me and I hate his overtly happy attitude to the point where I never want to see him. Why did the Absolute even make him come here? It could be…

"Shut up for a second," I say to stop his ramblings, "Maybe you were brought here so I can discover my heart's true ability!"

"I don't know. Don't you have to go to work and help take care of your family?"

"What's more important? Becoming my true self to serve the Absolute in the right way or constantly walking in circles?"

"Becoming your true self."

"Right. Besides, my parents don't need me."

"Yes, they do. You're their daughter."

"No, they never did. They only needed someone to make money for them," I say before ducking my head into my house to say to my mother, "Mother! I'm going out with Eleazar! We're going to find my heart's Absolute ability!"

"Good, good! Make your father and me proud," she says.

"Sure." Turning to Eleazar, I push him along and then say, "Come on, come on! Portal us out of here!"

"Okay, hold on."

A portal opens and on the other side, I can see a busy office. We go into it before the portal closes behind us.

Eleazar approaches the man dressed in gold like him that's sitting at the front desk and says, "Hey, Mr. Adivino."

"Back already, Eleazar? It's a good thing your portals gently push aside people and open in open spaces."

"It's all thanks to the Absolute."

"Sure is. Who is this with you? Your best friend that you talk about so much?"

"Yes, she is."

"Who is this?" I ask Eleazar.

"This is my advisor or rather an advisor or mystic for those with a Heart Absolute ability. He, along with the other mystics, have the Absolute ability to consult to Absolute typically to ask if a course of action is correct."

Great, another ability to be jealous of. If only it was so easy if me to get an answer to every question I have.

"So, you're going to ask if us going to find my heart's Absolute ability is correct?"

"Yep!"

"How long is this going to take?"

"This shouldn't take too long, young lady. Just be patient while I get the help of the other advisors."

Adivino goes away while I go find someplace to sit.

"I can show you around the place if you'd like, so you're not just waiting here," Eleazar says.

I take one look around the building to see all the people with fantastic Heart Absolute abilities such as turning objects into gold, sprouting wings from their back, and the ability to make copies of themselves. Not wanting to see other people's Heart Absolute abilities, I decline the offer then continue to look at people using their abilities regardless and daydream about what ability I'll get. My hope is that I get something different that's unique to me since two people having the same Heart Absolute ability while both are alive is incredibly rare. Maybe I'll be able to turn water into a solid substance, turn invisible, immediately clean things in the blink of an eye, or perhaps something simple like superhuman strength. I'll take almost anything as long as it gets me out of my current job and life situation.

From a distance, I can see Eleazar talking to one of his friends that can teleport objects from one place to another. I don't remember if he told me that she's related to him in any way or a distant relative since I hardly pay attention to what he says during his visits. It's also possible that she isn't related to him and her heart's ability is something new in her family, which I keep hoping is the case for me. Typically, a child will inherit one or a combination of their parent's or grandparent's abilities, but there are cases where a child or even multiple children in a family will have completely different abilities. Eleazar sees me looking over at him and his friends and motions for me to join them, but I shake my head. He then gets them to come over to me, the idiot.

"Everyone, this is my best friend, Cornelia. She's a really friendly person," Eleazar says.

Despite seeing the obvious sour expression on my face, Eleazar's friends still introduce themselves with smiles on their faces and tell me about what Eleazar said about me. Is having a sickeningly happy demeanor a requirement for working here? Also, what am I some kind of pet brought to a show in tell? Eleazar must've been telling many tall stories about me if everyone is fussing over me as if I'm some kind of celebrity.

"Eleazar, we've come to a decision," Adivino says as he comes back.

I push through the crowd of Eleazar's friends and ask, "What is it?"

"You are to go with him to learn about your Heart Absolute's ability by experiencing a few events that will teach you about it."

"Yes, yes! Finally!"

"This is great, Cornelia-"

"Come on and make a portal already! Come on!" I say as I grab Eleazar's arm and pull him out of his crowd of friends.

A portal opens in front of us and I try to get Eleazar to hurry up, but he's resisting as he says his goodbyes to his friends.

"You're her guiding light, Eleazar. Take good care that she learns what it really means to be herself and the true value of love, truth, and the Absolute," Adivino says.

"Don't worry, I will!" Eleazar says before going through the portal with me.

Finally, I'll be able to get my heart's Absolute ability and become truly myself. Then, I'll be able to live a happy and satisfying life.

Chapter 2 – Absolute or False

A blindly light subsides as I get through the portal to reveal a beautiful forest of flowers and wildlife.

"Huh. I thought we'd be in some kind of training place that will bring out my heart's Absolute ability," I say.

"Adivino did say that'd we experience events that will teach you. Maybe we're supposed to see how other people get their Heart Absolute ability so you can learn from them?" Eleazar suggests.

"I see how that could help, but still, how will we know what events to follow? Who are we going to follow and what exactly am I supposed to learn? This place looks and smells like a peaceful beautiful paradise."

"Yeah, but something about it doesn't feel right."

"I think you're just imagining things."

The sound of people moving draws our attention to a squad of knights that are moving through the forest. They must've not seen us because we're in the shadows of the trees and a fair distance away.

One of them looks around and then says, "Captain, shouldn't we look for Lionel? He's not here."

"If he's not here with us, he must've been enraptured by a trick of the witch in this forest. Simpleton couldn't even follow the order of staying close by us. The rest of you better stay close. We'll search for his corpse after our hunt is complete."

"Yes, sir," the knights say before moving on.

"Huh. There's a witch in this forest. Sounds like a fairy tale you tell children," I say.

"That's because fairy tales, like all fiction, are inspired by real life with some being based on more real things than others," Eleazar says.

"Right, and I'm assuming you still believe in the monsters under your bed that give you sleep paralysis and try to drag you under when you're awake when you're not supposed to."

"I still believe that."

"Of course you do."

Eleazar and I hear the sound of someone running in armor from behind us and turn around to see a young man in armor with the symbol of a royal blue sheep crest on his chest, which is the same symbol the other knights had.

"Have you seen-" the boy says before I cut him off by saying, "Your knight friends who've abandoned you? Yes, we have."

"They haven't abandoned me! They would never."

"I'm sorry, but your captain told them to. You must be Lionel. My name is Eleazar," Eleazar says.

"So, you must be telling the truth, if you've heard my name. Yes, my name is Lionel. Nice to meet you Eleazar. I can't believe my friends would leave me behind."

"They said you must've been enraptured by the witch of this forest. Are you okay? Were you under some kind of spell?"

"No, I wasn't. I was just distracted by the beauty of the forest as if it spoke to me like it usually does."

"So, you were enraptured," I say.

"I guess you could say so since the witch made the forest and I do love nature. Don't you? The beauty of nature is so alluring that I could stare at and talk to it all day."

"You do that a lot, Cornelia," Eleazar mentions.

"I don't do the speaking to the forest part." What kind of weirdos do that anyway? "You better get back to your so-called friends, Lionel."

"I can't do that and leave you, civilians, alone without protection. I'll escort you out of the forest before rejoining my squad."

"I'm afraid that we can't do that," I say, "The Absolute led us here so I can get my Heart Absolute ability."

"Oh, really? That's amazing! I wish I had my heart's Absolute ability. In that way, I could help more people."

Eleazar says, "Well, you can help us by helping us get to your friends. Cornelia is meant to view some event here to help her and she may have to witness you and your friends defeating this witch."

"Okay! Let's do that!" As Lionel accompanies us while we walk in the direction of his squad, he asks us, "What do you guys do?"

"I help teleport people around the world," Eleazar says.

"That explains those fancy robes of yours. What about you, Cornelia?"

"Nothing good. I just work in community service."

"I did that before I became a knight and even after becoming a soldier, I had to be the cleaning guy for everything at the base since I didn't do so good in my exams to become a knight. In retrospect, I feel like I should've stayed a community service member."

"You're stupid for thinking that."

"I know." Huh. I didn't expect him to agree with me. "I should trust the Absolute where it takes me because it is the Absolute after. It's literally the truth and doesn't lie to me, right?"

"Right, I'm sure you'll eventually become a great knight. You just started out after all," Eleazar says.

"You're right. Thanks, Eleazar and Cornelia."

What did I say that was encouraging for him? Whatever. We continue through the forest and as we adventure forward, the forest grows and changes ahead of us with pretty plants and flowers and smells directing us to go in certain directions.

"Should we follow the way that's being presented to us? Maybe the witch is trying to guide us to the knights?" I suggest.

"No, because the witch is conceited," Lionel says, "This power of hers isn't natural nor is she being her true self. I doubt she is a nice person."

"Why's that? We haven't been attacked and this place looks beautiful."

"Being conceited doesn't make you a good person because you choose to become something that isn't you and you put yourself above the Absolute because you think you

know better than truth itself. How can anyone that's like

that be good?"

I guess that makes sense. We were taught in school

that by the end of our lives our hearts will be judged on

how closely they resemble the Absolute since all hearts are

made in the image of it and all hearts yearn to be what they

were meant to be whether they acknowledge it or not.

Hearts become conceited when they reject the Absolute or

willfully ignore the call to learn the truth about themselves

and the reality of the world around us. If a heart is

blackened by conceit, it is tossed away to be forgotten, but

if a heart closely resembles the Absolute, it will be cleaned

of stain before being forever remembered and join the

many hearts gathered in the Absolute to live forever

happily in its love. Of course, I've tried to be what the

Absolute wants me to be though I don't really know why

some people who are viewed as conceited are viewed as

bad since they are trying to be what they believe to be themselves and this forest doesn't look like it's the home of an evil witch.

After going in our own direction for a while, we find the knights who seem to be on edge and it seems like one or two of their number is missing.

"Captain!" Lionel says.

"Lionel, be careful you, idiot!" the captain says.

"I am, sir!"

"Obviously not since you brought civilians deeper into this forest."

"They're here because of the Absolute and Cornelia here needs to witness something to get her Heart Absolute ability."

"Okay, whatever, there's nothing we can do to get them out of the forest now. Just keep your eyes open. Two of our knights disappeared even though they were close to us. Since you managed to make your way back, we're hoping they'll find their way back as well."

"I hope they'll find their way back too, sir."

"Shut up and form up!"

"Yes, sir! Come on, Cornelia and Eleazar. We'll protect you."

As we get in the middle of the squad of knights who move forward with their backs to us, we hear a woman's voice echo in the forest. She says, "Beware, all trespassers. Leave me in peace or suffer the consequences."

Soon after, two sets of broken knight armor fly at us with presumably the wearers following behind them. They scream in terror in their damaged clothes as they run away from us and tell us to run with them out of the forest because of the witch. Maybe they have the right idea.

"We won't run away from you, witch. You'll pay for your conceited behavior, your thievery, and the many lives you've taken," Lionel bravely says.

"You should leave with your friends, boy. I'll spare you for your appreciation of my garden. Take the offer."

"No! I am duty bound to bring you to justice."

"Then you will soon regret not accepting my mercy."

The trees of the forest suddenly have thorns growing around them and husks made of thorns that look like soldiers with swords and spears rise from the ground to attack us. Lionel and the knights try fighting these forest soldiers; however, they are unable to put them down since the forest soldiers keep moving even when their heads and legs are cut off, and the parts that are cut off are replaced by thorns that come from the ground. In a desperate attempt to kill one of these soldiers, the captain repeatedly slashes it apart until it's all destroyed. This would've inspired the rest of the knights to do the same, but he is dragged away screaming into the forest by a large bush of thorns.

As everyone scatters, Lionel says, "We must stand together! Stop running away!"

Unfortunately for us, the knights run away together and are now ignored by the forest knights for some reason. Eleazar tries to make a portal but is unable to and confirms it by saying so. What am I supposed to do now? Is my Heart Absolute ability going to appear now? Come on! Appear already! This would be the perfect opportunity for it. It would be storybook if it does and the answer to my prayers that I've been waiting for. We're surrounded by the forest soldiers now with no way out and Lionel is exhausted and injured from the fighting. My Heart Absolute ability just has to appear now!

Lionel is knocked to the ground and struggles to get up. He says, "No! I'm not going to let anyone else under my protection die."

As Lionel slams his sword down defiantly, all the forest soldiers stop moving, which saves him from almost being killed by them. Something has changed about him.

My eyes feel like they're telling me this, but I'm not sure

what it is. Could it be possible? Lionel holds out his hand

and flowers appear on the bodies of the forest soldier and

they all back away as he holds out his hands. No way…

"It's not possible," I hear the witch's voice echo in

the forest.

"My heart's inner ability has awoken thanks to the

Absolute. It's over for you now that I am able to control the

forest. Give up and submit yourself to justice," Lionel says.

"There is no such thing as justice. That is why I do

what I do. This isn't over yet. Not while my heart still gives

me power over a portion of the forest you don't control."

"Come on, Eleazar and Cornelia. I'll protect you as

we move forward," Lionel says.

More forest soldiers with flowers on them form

around us that act as our guards. The forest around us also

changes as the thorns around the trees retract back into the ground.

"I'm so glad that you got your Heart Absolute ability, Lionel," Eleazar says.

"I am too, especially since I needed it now more than ever to protect you guys. We're not too far from the witch now. The forest tells me so," Lionel says.

How come I wasn't the one to get the ability to control plants in the forest? Don't get me wrong, I'm glad that Lionel got his Heart Absolute ability in time to save us, but still. Oh, and now the wildlife in the forest, the squirrels, birds, rabbits, and deer are here to help us too. Why not? I'm assuming Lionel getting this ability is something I was supposed to see. So, what am I exactly supposed to take away from this? Well, this isn't over yet, so the answer should be becoming clearer soon.

With Lionel, Eleazar and I finally come across the witch with a small squad of her own forest soldiers behind her. She doesn't look like the ugly witch I imagined her to be. Instead, she looks to be a young woman about my age dressed in gold, black, and green grass and flowers with a crown made of black and gold plants. The only part of her that looks like what I imagined is the black heart-shaped hole in her chest, her black and green eyes, and her crown because the conceited are said to always crown themselves with whatever type of crown they feel they deserve.

"Let go of your control of the forest. Can't you hear its cries of pain as it tries to escape your grasp?" Lionel says.

"I don't hear it. Besides, control of the forest is a power I rightly deserve after all the suffering I've been through and the charity I provide," the witch says.

"What charity do you provide? You attack the Church dedicated to the Absolute and everyone who enters your forest."

"I've only attacked those who've wronged me and those who will harm me and those I love. What your leaders haven't told you was that I sought the Church's help to save my dying family, but even after so many years of serving them as a gardener and house cleaner, they wouldn't take care of my family because I couldn't afford the bills for their constant care. I had to rely on becoming a witch and being so-called conceited to give them a home out here and the care they needed until they peacefully died."

For some reason, Lionel kneels down and the grass reaches out from the ground and wraps around his hands. More grass from behind him reaches up and around his eyes.

"What are you doing?" I ask him.

"They're buried here, right?" Lionel asks the witch.

"Yes, is nature telling you this?"

"It is."

"Then you must also be able to speak to their souls. They'll tell you how much they love me and how I was right to do what I was doing." An odd silence fills the air while Lionel looks surprised and worried. "Well, am I right?"

"No. They feel cold…I can hardly hear their voices."

"What?"

"They're in the Land of the Forgotten where all lies and falsehoods reside. You made their hearts conceited like yours, didn't you?"

"They agreed what I did was right. I punished those who wronged us, took what was rightfully ours, and protected us from people who would want to hurt us for doing so."

"It doesn't matter if you were wronged. You still turned their hearts into conceited, false ones and because of that, they'll suffer for all eternity."

"No, that can't be true! They talk to me from time to time to tell me how happy they are!"

"Those must be the vainglory, demons in the image of your family talking to you. They were the ones who helped make your heart conceited and the same ones who made the hearts of those in the Church who wronged you conceited as well. If you continue as you are, you'll join them and your family in the Land of the Forgotten."

"No, no, no! You're lying and you'll pay for that!"

The two armies of forest soldiers and their leaders clash. While this is happening, roots come up from the ground and surround us, which have presumably come from Lionel. I can see Lionel and the witch fighting and yelling things at each other but can't exactly hear what they're saying in all this fighting. Eventually, the dust settles with Lionel being the victor and the witch at the end of his blade.

"I know what it's like to fail those who you want to protect. When my brother and I were out hunting, I failed to protect him. Instead, I ran away and left him to be food for the wolves. I've also failed my squad and the civilians I was tasked with protecting on multiple occasions. I feel like a failure because of those I've lost even if I was still victorious in the end."

"Why are you telling me this? Why not just kill me and be done with your mission?"

"Because I've felt the torturing cold of the Land of the Forgotten and I want to protect you from that horrible fate."

"Protect me? You don't have a reason to do that. What kind of knight doesn't kill a witch like me?"

"One that wants to protect rather than kill. As far as I'm concerned, killing is a last resort option and I don't ever want to kill anyone from now on, especially with what

I've felt from the Land of the Forgotten and now that my Heart Absolute will allow me to take people in alive."

"Even so, I'm a conceited witch. There's no hope for me to change."

"Of course you can. Everyone is capable of redemption since we all make mistakes. Trust me, I should know. I'll help you change if you let me."

Looking at him with a puzzled look, the witch pushes Lionel's blade away from her throat and then says, "Okay, fine. I believe you. Take me in."

"I will, but first, let me erase this façade you've created and give back the forest its natural beauty."

As he says this, Lionel puts his hand on the ground and the beautiful forest around us decays and dies but then is quickly replaced by a somehow more beautiful forest than the previous one that overtakes it and fills it with more plant life and even more varieties of wildlife teeming in it. Seeing this stuns the witch and her appearance changes to something more humble as she is now wearing a simple dress made of grass and her crown is gone. It looks to me that she's no longer conceited. Eleazar screams in joyous excitement and hugs me because of the occasion while I look in awe as to what Lionel managed to do.

"Amazing…" the witch says.

"Now, are you ready to go?" Lionel asks.

"Yes."

"Hold on, guys. I'll make this journey quicker for you," Eleazar says before making a portal.

This portal leads us to a simple small city with a castle in the center and walls around it like most cities that I've heard of. People in the streets are shocked by our sudden appearance and it seems like the guards in the city are even more shocked to see Lionel taking in the witch by himself.

While we watch them talk to the guards, Eleazar puts his hand on my shoulder and then says, "Ah, don't you love happy endings?"

"This isn't the end for them. It's just the beginning of a new struggle. Lionel will probably fight more because of his Heart Absolute ability and the witch will have to serve time in jail," I say.

"Don't be so cynical. I'm sure things will be for the better for both of them."

"Sure."

Lionel and the witch turn around to us.

"Thanks for everything, Eleazar and Cornelia," Lionel says.

"Thank you for protecting us and congratulations on a job well done," Eleazar says.

"It's my pleasure. I hope we see each other again someday."

"Me too."

"Cornelia is it?" the witch asks me.

"Yes?" I say.

"I recognize the look on your face. I've had it my entire life and know how you feel just by looking at you. Don't take the same path I did or else you might end up hurting those you love."

"Sure. Thanks for the advice."

Thanks, but no thanks. There's no one I really love so there's no chance of me doing what she said. The two then say their goodbyes before walking away from us.

"So, what have you learned?" Eleazar asks me.

"Nothing in particular other than I'd like to have a similar ability to Lionel's," I say.

"Oh, come on. There was a lot to learn from what we witnessed even though they were reminders of things we learned in school."

"Well, do you want to take a rest before we go to the next place?"

"No, I want to keep going."

"Okay, if you say so."

There was hardly anything for me to learn from that besides what I already knew about Absolute and conceited hearts. Maybe it'll all make sense when I've seen everything I need to. Now more than ever I'm anxious to get my Heart Absolute ability. Eleazar forms a portal and we head off to our next destination.

Chapter 3 - Law Enforcement vs Assault

Our portal takes us to the entrance of a grand cathedral decorated with statues of serviles or angels. The statues of serviles on one side wear robes and hold a book in one hand and a shield in the other while the statues on the other side are wearing armor and hold swords in one hand and a weighing scale in the other hand. Two big crowds of people are gathering at the cathedral all of which seem to be nobility judging by their outfits. One group of these people almost seem to be wearing a type of light armor that's colored crimson and black while the other one is dressed more elegantly in lighter colors of white, gold, and shades of light blue.

"Oh! I'm so glad that we managed to get here!" Eleazar says as he grabs my hand and hurries us into the cathedral.

"Why? Do you know what's going on?" I ask.

"Two friends of mine are going to be crowned today. Let's hurry!"

I guess it shouldn't surprise me that Eleazar got invited to this wedding since he's done much for many nobles and Church leadership. The guards recognize Eleazar, don't bother checking to see if we have an invitation like they do with the rest of the guests, and bring us to a special balcony to get a good view of what's happening. Eventually, the ceremony begins and I follow Eleazar and everyone's conduct so I can do what I'm supposed to and not stick out more than I already do. During the ceremony, I hear the names of Eleazar's two friends that this ceremony is for, Prince Caleb and Princess Kyla.

Prince Caleb wears a suit of spiky crimson and black armor. In contrast, Princess Kyla wears a silky dress light blue and white dress. Both are crowned by an archbishop who blesses them and then hovers his hands over them.

"Prince Caleb and Princess Kyla, I charge you with protecting our home, the Kingdom of Simbiosi. Through your unity and the power of your hearts, you will serve the Absolute, truth and love itself, and do what's best for your neighbors, your family, and strangers alike. Such will be your responsibility until your death," the archbishop says.

After this, a normal mass is held. Being a noble restricts your life choices more than being a peasant like me. If I ran off and had a plan as to where, my parents and my boss can do really do nothing about it. It's not illegal for a nobody like me to run away since I'm so replaceable.

On the other hand, if a noble runs away, their families send their personal forces or the authorities to get them. It's illegal, in most cases, for a noble to leave their given job because of their importance and they face harsh jail sentences once someone is available to replace them. There are even stories made about these kinds of nobles. One story I remember is about a princess who sought Our Lady of Sorrows to become holy.

Huh? Oh, the mass is over. I got too distracted in my thoughts to really pay attention to it. Anyways, Eleazar and I go to the celebration for the prince and princess and get to talk to them.

Eleazar hugs both of them and says, "I'm so glad that I made it to your ceremony."

"We're glad too," Kyla says.

"It's good to see you, so is this your girlfriend that you always talk about?" Caleb asks.

"I'm not his girlfriend! What are you telling people?!" I say to Eleazar.

"Nothing! I didn't say that."

"I'm just joking. He does always talk about you so I assume you were. My apologies."

He should stop talking about me to everyone he meets. I'm already sick of it.

"So, why did the Absolute bring you here?" Kyla asks.

"Cornelia is supposed to witness certain events so that she can unlock her heart's Absolute ability."

"I'm hoping to get it soon so I can leave the life I currently live."

"What kind of ability are you hoping to get?" Caleb asks.

"Something great, something amazing like transforming things, making things manifest, and stuff like that you know. An ability that stories are made of."

"I get it. Having an amazing Heart Absolute ability is a blessing. We should know since we have one of the best as we can summon dragons," Kyla says.

"I summon a better dragon though. It's a red and black dragon that's the embodiment of justice," Caleb says.

"It's not a better dragon. It's just a complimentary dragon to mine, which is a light blue and white dragon that's the embodiment of mercy."

"Those do sound amazing. I definitely want something like that."

"It's great to have, but you also bear an even greater responsibility to use it well. Believe it or not, I sometimes feel jealous for community service workers like you, so I could live a simple, humble, and quiet life."

"I don't feel that way, most of the time anyway. The only time I do is when I want to be left alone, not have so much responsibility hanging over my head, and people bothering me with things I already know."

"You might actually get an ability that will help you in your current job. That's what happens with most people and what happened with us. Our dragons help us deal mercy and justice just like we do on a daily basis."

"I hope not. I'll lose my mind if that's the case."

It better not happen. I don't want one of those "you had your special power this whole time" sort of cases. I will go insane if it does. Both Eleazar and Kyla tell me about the honors of community service that I roll my eyes at.

"Our maids and butlers hold some of the highest honors in our family and are invited to our many dinners and celebrations. When they fall sick or are dying, they are given the best service we can offer and their families are compensated after their deaths," Kyla explains.

Blah, blah, blah, I don't care. I don't even care if Kyla and Caleb offer me the chance to clean their castles and take care of their families. All I want is out of this job. For the rest of the celebration, I stay quiet and enjoy whatever kinds of exquisite foods they serve except for the healthier stuff.

"You have to eventually eat your greens and healthy foods," Eleazar tells me.

With a mouth full of chicken and beef, I say, "Whatever."

Back home, I eat enough mediocre foods and force myself to eat my greens and fruits. I'm going to enjoy all the meat I can while I'm here.

"She has the right idea," Caleb says with his thumbs up towards me.

Kyla shakes her head in response. After dinner, people start to dance. Knowing what's going to happen, I try to get up and use going to the bathroom as an excuse to skip out on dancing, but Eleazar already knows I'm lying and drags me to the dance floor to dance with him, which embarrasses me to no end. Kyla drags Caleb to the dance floor to dance with us and he feels the same way I do.

Eventually, the dancing ends, we have dessert, and the party ends. Caleb and Kyla allow us to rest in their castle which has a similar design to the cathedral we were at. Apparently, this place is usually used as a meeting place for both sides of the kingdom and the home of the newly appointed prince and princess who are meant to oversee both sides of it.

What doesn't surprise me is that Caleb and Kyla are married. On the other hand, what does surprise me is how they got this castle and their new responsibility. Their families had to raise up a single heir who would find someone on the other side of the kingdom to fall in love with. Assuming this happened, the couples would compete for the position Caleb and Kyla have now. The rest of the details are lost to me as I passively listen to them talk to Eleazar who probably already knows this. Well, at least they give me another reason not to feel jealous about nobles.

Albert Oon

Tonight, Eleazar and I are given one of the guest

rooms to sleep in, which is meant to fit around twenty or so

people. I sleep on the other side of the room because I don't

want to be bothered as much by Eleazar's snoring. When

we used to have sleepovers, he would snore and keep me

up for an hour before I fell asleep. At first, I thought it was

funny until it quickly got old and annoying. In the morning,

the castle's servants wake us up and give us new clothes.

Eleazar is given a clean pair of his uniform while I am

given the same clothes that the servants are wearing. This

pair of clothes is colored light blue and crimson with

designs of golden flowers on them. Since these clothes are

nicer than what I have, I wear them.

The servants then bring us to the luxurious dinner

table that looks like it's meant to fit at least fifty people.

Here, the servants are eating with Kyla and Caleb and the

table is filled with many kinds of breakfast meals such as

plates full of pancakes and plates that have breakfast

sandwiches with a side serving of potatoes. We are given seats by Kyla and Caleb who ask us how our rest was and how is the service here.

"The service is great and I slept well, at least until Cornelia started her snoring like she usually does," Eleazar says.

"I do not snore," I say.

"To be honest, I miss it. She did it all the time when we had sleepovers and I find it cute."

"Shut up."

"I know how you feel. Caleb does it all the time too," Kyla says.

"Shut up. I do not snore," Caleb argues.

"Anyways, what do you think you'll be doing to help Cornelia find her Heart Absolute ability today?"

"I thought we keep following you since you already have yours and we were brought to you by the Absolute."

"You won't be able to do that today since Caleb and I are already tasked with taking down the Kingdom of the Universale."

"That is unless you can handle the danger," Caleb adds.

"Why are you going after them?" I ask.

"They're heretics who have openly attacked and rebelled against our Church."

"Still, why attack them? I've heard that their kingdom accepts people of all beliefs."

"That's exactly the problem," Caleb says, "They accept the conceited and all that is false thinking that what's true or not doesn't matter as long as you appear to be a good person. Truth and lies cannot coexist, especially in a society where the good of humanity means something different to different people. Love of one thing always leads to hatred of the opposite."

War, Love, and the Absolute

I've heard of Caleb and Kyla's Kingdom of Simbiosi always going to war with defectors and supposed heretical kingdoms.

"Why not try to convince them to change? Why go to war?"

"War is what we're good at when people refuse to give us what is rightfully due. It's the reality of this world. Kingdoms and people are constantly at war for what's God of their hearts and only those who fight for the Absolute will have the final victory. Don't worry about the casualties. Our dragons will rightly judge the Universale, spare the innocent, and execute the guilty."

He's not lying or exaggerating. There are always people fighting in this world for something they highly value. I still don't like that Caleb and Kyla will have to go after the Universale. I've heard they're such nice people and have Heart Absolute abilities. What does it matter if they're slightly wrong about their beliefs?

"Whatever the reason for this war is, Cornelia and I can join you. We already put ourselves in danger before coming here to witness a great man obtain his Heart Absolute ability and change someone else's heart in the process. If we're not meant to be there, the Absolute will let me make a portal to get us out of there," Eleazar says.

"Okay. Stay behind us and out of danger as much as you can," Kyla says.

"Or maybe they or at least Cornelia should be in more danger. It is the way that a lot of people get their ability. It's how we got it when we risked our lives to save each other and almost died in the process," Caleb mentions.

"That's true, but I don't think she'll have to go through the same thing. She doesn't have the same responsibilities as us."

"You don't know that. She may obtain some kind of amazing ability in battle."

War, Love, and the Absolute

"You think that because you think of everything in terms of battles."

"That's right because life is one constant battle against vices and our enemies."

Again, Caleb is right and I hope he's correct about me getting an amazing ability in the coming battle. When we head out, I ride with Caleb while Eleazar rides with Kyla since the dragons can't really handle more than two people on them and Kyla doesn't mind me riding with Caleb who I like more. Eleazar creates a portal for us and we go through it to instantly get to where we need to be. We find ourselves a fair distance away from a city with large city walls and many castles within it, which makes it look like a city controlled by kings. The city is surrounded by damaged farmlands that look more like a forgotten warzone than anything resembling a quiet farm town. Further from the warzone are luscious fields that show the beauty that the warzone probably was.

While we fly to the city, I notice that we aren't being fired upon, so I say to Caleb, "They aren't attacking us. Maybe they want peace?"

"We do too, but they refuse it. If they aren't going to fire the first shot, then we will," Caleb says.

His and Kyla's dragons start firing a barrage of red and blue fireballs respectively at the city that damage the walls, castles, and churches. This is when the inhabitants of the city send fireballs of their own at us and leads to us firing at them while advancing and dodging their counterattacks. We spin, roll, and fly in all kinds of ways to dodge the attacks, which also make me feel sick. As we fly over the city walls, the barrage stops.

"We wish to negotiate terms of surrender," someone says from the balcony of one of the castles.

This person seems to be a noble because of their clothing though they are not too well dressed and there's no sign of them being conceited. They don't have a crown or any black shaped hole in their chest that would show regardless of their clothes. Caleb's dragon bathes this person in its red fire that overwhelms their person to their knees but doesn't burn them. In fact, their clothes don't even burn off.

"See? I have submitted myself to your fire and have come out unscathed. It proves my innocence. Now, if you will, please meet us on the ground to talk. We don't want to continue this war."

Caleb and Kyla look at each other.

"Okay, we'll do it," Kyla says.

We land on the ground where we meet many others who look like the noble all of which are modestly dressed. Again, Caleb's dragon breathes fire on these people and again they are unaffected by it, but everything around them, on the other hand, catches fire and is put out by the people around us.

"Do you not yet see that we are innocent?" one of the people asks.

"It appears to be so. Prove it with your formal surrender and what penance you will do to pay for your crimes against the Church and Simbiosi," Caleb says.

"We have done nothing wrong."

"Oh yeah? That battlefield outside of your walls and the many you have injured say otherwise."

"We were defending ourselves!"

"I don't believe heretics who preach against the Church and make us look like liars."

"We don't believe you are liars. We just think you're mistaken."

"Enough! Clearly, you don't really want to surrender or repent of your sins. If my dragon won't burn you, then perhaps Kyla's will." Caleb motions to Kyla and she reluctantly nods back and her dragon breathes its fire on the people in front of us leading to the same result.

"Huh? A bunch of fireproof fellas, aren't you?"

"We aren't! We know that those flames burn the guilty and no suit of armor is strong enough to resist it."

"Then it's some kind of conceited magic."

"Look at us. We wear no crowns or clothe ourselves in kingly clothes. In fact, our hearts have their Absolute ability."

"Prove it."

Two people step up from the group and two dragons manifest beside them that appear to be just like the dragons Caleb and Kyla have. They are surprised by this and speak to each other in whispers that I can't hear. I'm just as concerned as they are. It's not common for those on the side of the Absolute to fight each other, but when it does, it historically ends in stalemates, and many innocent people dead. It could also be that the Universale are actually faking their Heart Absolute abilities and their innocence through some kind of conceited ability though I don't think this is the case.

"Forget it. We came here to punish your rebellion and since you aren't going to surrender, then you will die," Caleb says as he takes out his spear and shield from his back.

He and his dragon charge at the two who have dragons. In response, they have their dragons breathe their fire on him and his. As Kyla moves to aid Caleb with her hammers and dragon, we get to cover. The other two dragons manage to push back Kyla, Caleb, and their dragons and even singe them with their fire. Undeterred by this, Kyla and Caleb fight on and manage to get in close to their enemies. Even the dragons fight together, though it seems like no side is winning.

"We should do something," I say.

"Like what? I'm trying to make a portal but can't."

"No, don't make a portal. Maybe my Heart Absolute ability will kick in soon."

Come on! Here's another chance for me to do something and it's still not coming out! Am I supposed to be learning something from this? If so, I don't see what it is just like the other time. Eventually, Kyla and Caleb are pushed back and seem to be on the edge of defeat. They get on their dragons and try to fight their enemies this way, which causes their enemies to do the same. This results in both sides taking flight and having them fight with their dragons in the sky. Some of the buildings are hit as a result of them exchanging fire blasts and debris fall down to where we are. The guards of the city protect us and the civilians before getting us to smaller buildings that they've made into shelters for fights like this, but it doesn't last long as both Caleb's and Kyla's dragons crash with them on it into the shelter.

Everyone in the shelter who isn't injured scatters while Eleazar and I pick ourselves up to check on Caleb and Kyla who are pretty banged up. Caleb's spikey armor is heavily damaged with the spikes missing, his left shoulder piece broken, and many places on his armor are damaged and burned. Meanwhile, Kyla's light armor which was once as white as snow is now dirtied and ruined with no trace of light blue or white left in it.

"Caleb! Kyla! Are you alright?" Eleazar says.

"Yeah, I'm fine enough to fight," Caleb says as he struggles to hold his spear and broken shield.

"No, you're not. We should find a place to hide and then plan out our next attack," Kyla says.

"Eleazar. Let the Absolute decide through your portals."

"I've been trying to make them. Maybe now they'll work."

War, Love, and the Absolute

A portal does end up appearing in front of us that we all go into. It puts us somewhere in an empty abandoned church that's in a not too crowded part of the city. Both Caleb's and Kyla's dragons disappear in a flash of light as they sit down to rest. Caleb punches the floor.

"What wrong?" Kyla asks.

"I thought we would easily win! We have our Heart Absolute abilities after all and we serve the truth, right? So, why didn't we win like we did the other times? What did we do wrong?" Caleb says.

"I don't know. This church that the Absolute brought us to may have an answer."

"I think that it shows us that we were right. This place used to be dedicated to the Absolute judging from the torn artworks and broken statues. What are we missing?"

"Maybe we're meant to think that the church isn't right about everything and a change in thinking may be in order. This church is abandoned after all," I suggest.

"How could you suggest that? We're fighting against an enemy whose beliefs contradict a need for truth since they accept all beliefs without care if those beliefs contradict one another, if they're based in historical and theological fact, and if they're reasonable."

"Maybe the Absolute is trying to show us that you're missing a part of the truth," Eleazar suggests.

"How so?" Kyla asks.

"This church does have signs of the worship of the Absolute present, but most of it is gone or torn down. Just like it, Caleb is talking all about your victories rather than the victories that the Absolute gave you. It is because of the Absolute that you have these abilities and they don't always guarantee you victory. Think about it like the job of an artist, writer, or any other job. You aren't perfect at the job, to begin with, and even when you're good at it, there's always room for improvement. I mean we aren't perfect people in our personalities either and we need the daily

help of the Absolute to become who we're meant to be."

"He's got a point," Caleb admits, "I do always resort

to violence first and then ask questions later, but I do it

because I want to protect the ones I love and establish

peace as quickly as I can."

"Peace is hard fought and won. It's a lesson I

struggle to learn too since my family and I try to negotiate

and covert our enemies sometimes to no avail. A firm,

correcting, and loving hand is required in those cases."

"And when there's a chance of conversion and

possibility to lessen the bloodshed, we have to restrain

ourselves."

Something about Caleb and Kyla changes. It's like

what happened to Lionel, but different though I just like

before, I can't tell what it is. The two of them summon their

dragons and allow us to ride with them to the primary

castle in the center of the city. Here, we approach the main gate and its many guards that defend it. Okay, what are you two going to do now?

"Prince Caleb and Princess Kyla of the Kingdom of Simbiosi, have you finally come to negotiate terms of peace?" a guard says.

Many more guards gather around us, the nobles in the castle gather at the windows and the other two who could summon dragons appear and guard the gate. Caleb and Kyla look at each other and then hold each other's hands. Now, something's really different about them. I can feel it and it looks like everyone around us can too judging from their reactions.

"We have come to bring both mercy and justice," Caleb and Kyla say in unison, "Both are part of a whole as we are with the Absolute and each other. The two are made into one flesh. Mercy and justice are nothing more than the Judgment of the Absolute."

Both of their dragons combine into a singular massive dragon. It's colored crimson, light blue, white, and black, has eight arms, four wings, and has other aspects of the dragons that make it up such as spiky horns and shield-like wings. The dragon roars before firing a blast of gold and black fire into the sky. A few seconds pass before the sky darkens and fire begins to rain from the sky. This fire homes in onto people and burns them with its flames. It exposes some as being conceited such as the two guards who had dragons under their control.

The dragon then breathes its fire into the ground to expose a large creature beneath it that begins to rise from the ground. This causes massive damage to the city and buildings to collapse. What's even stranger about all this is that certain people are caught by the black tendrils of whatever is beneath here and sucked into it. Eleazar and I struggle to keep our balance until he's able to make us a portal and get us out of the city. His portal brings us far away from the city, but still close enough to see what's going on.

What's before us now is even more insane than everything that's going on. A black mass of faces and mini arms rises from the ground and levitates through some unknown means. Caleb and Kyla's new dragon flies around this massive being and I can hardly see them on it.

In an echoing mass of male and female voices, the being says, "You have your Absolute, your truth and we have ours. This is its manifestation as a result of our unification and all our hearts combined. This is our True Absolute. Make peace with our god now or face its judgment."

Caleb's and Kyla's voices ring out as one as well and respond, "There are no multiple truths. Only one. Let the Absolute's judgment come upon you to deliver both mercy and justice."

War, Love, and the Absolute

Both Caleb and Kyla's dragon fly around the being

breathing fire around it to destroy it as its many faces and

arms lung out to try to stop them. I feel so small compared

to everything around me as if I shrunk to the size of an ant.

I've heard of people using their Heart Absolute abilities

together as one to make a new power, but I didn't imagine

it would be like this. It makes me think about what my

Heart Absolute ability will look like and what I'm

supposed to learn from this. Maybe it's that I should

remember that the Absolute is the source of my Heart

Absolute ability and I won't be perfect even with it? The

first part of it goes without saying since the ability is called

a Heart Absolute ability after all, but the second part is

harder to find relevant.

So what if I won't be instantly perfect? I'll have my

Heart Absolute ability, my life will change for the better,

and things will progressively get better from there. I

imagine that I'll be like Caleb and Kyla. Right now,

they've just finished off the being that is crumbling to the ground in burning pieces. They've gone from achievement to achievement with probably more in the future. Eleazar cheers for their victory and I put my hand in his face so he doesn't hug me in excitement.

"Aren't you happy for them?" Eleazar asks.

"Sure. Just portal them and us out of here. They probably want to go home and celebrate their victory," I say.

After agreeing with me, we meet up with Caleb and Kyla and portal back home to find everyone overjoyed at the news of our victory. It is then that their dragon becomes two separate dragons again, which doesn't bother them too much since they'll probably be able to use it again. A victory celebration like the one we were at the other day is held the next day and Eleazar and I attend it or rather Eleazar forces me to attend it since he doesn't want to portal us out to our next destination. At the celebration, much praise is said for Caleb and Kyla who are allowed to speak after they receive their gifts from the nobles of Simbiosi and Church leaders.

"Our victory may have been won, but we still have a long road ahead," Kyla says as she starts off her speech, "The world is a violent place. Having mercy on criminals and sinners is the preferred option to deal with these people since we are all flawed, but sometimes justice must be satiated."

"But even then, justice is mercy because it stops a person from ruining themselves further and makes them see the error of their ways. Every sin and evil deed is supposed to be rewarded with the soul's death and bodily death, and yet, hardly anyone is struck down where they stand immediately after they sin. No matter how much we improve and get strong, we still have room for improvement and it's in that space that the Absolute continues to inspire us and mold us into who we are meant to become."

Caleb and Kyla then say with one voice, "Through the trials and hardships of life, we will overcome our faults. Together with our hearts beating as one, we will become truly ourselves and establish peace in the world through mercy and justice."

Their speech receives the applause of everyone in the hall. The celebration goes on for the entire night and exhausts me to the point where I don't feel like I have the strength to continue for the next day. I wish Eleazar didn't make me dance so much and try all the food. Stupid idiot. Eventually, after breakfast the next day, we say our goodbyes and leave.

"You're in a rush," Eleazar says.

"Yes, I am. Now, make a portal," I say.

"Didn't you enjoy your time here?"

"Eleazar, please, the next place we are going to will give me the last piece of the puzzle that I need to obtain my heart's Absolute ability. Can we hurry up?!"

"Okay, okay. Someone didn't get enough sleep."

If he wasn't my only way to get where I need to go, I'd punch him in the face. I'm surprised that I haven't done it after so many years. Finally, he makes a portal that I immediately go through. Now, I'll get the last thing I need to unlock my Heart Absolute ability, and then I'll truly become who I'm meant to be and start a new and better life.

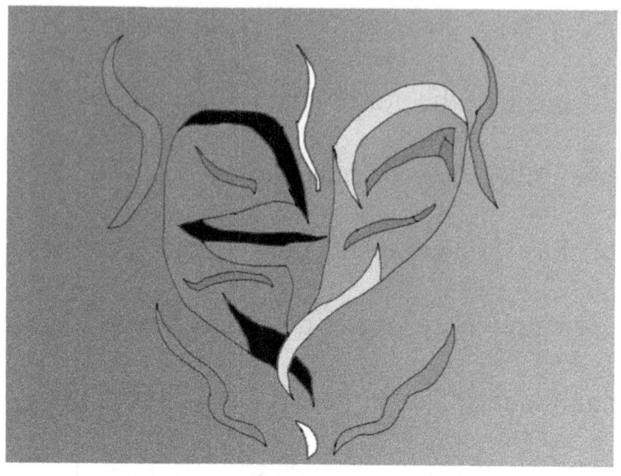

Chapter 4 - Amazing Things in Plain Sight

Rushing through the portal, I find myself in a strange place. It's not a beautiful forest or a grand city. It's just a simple farm town similar to the one I'm from. We're standing in someone's backyard where their horses, cows, and chickens are eating and going about their daily business.

"What is this?" I ask.

"A backyard," Eleazar says with a sarcastic smile.

Okay, that's it.

"Ow! Why did you slap the back of my head for?"

"Because."

Once the portal behind us closes, the animals start freaking out for whatever reason.

"What a way to start the morning," a girl about my age says as she exits the backdoor, "Hey! You two better clean up this mess you made or I will chase you down and make you pay!"

Eleazar and I help her calm down the animals and put them back in their proper places out of a sense of obligation. I'd rather not start any trouble in this town before we find whoever we're supposed to.

"Now, what are you two doing here? Explain yourselves before I call the guards," the girl asks.

"My best friend, Cornelia, here is on a quest to find her Heart Absolute ability and this is the final destination where she's meant to witness something to help her. My name is Eleazar and it's nice to meet you. What's your name?"

"It doesn't matter. Go on your quest and-"

"Miquita! Be kind to these strangers. Don't you see that the young man is a noble?" a woman inside the house says.

"So what?"

"So, invite them in and let them eat breakfast with us."

"Okay, mother. Come in."

We take the offer even though we just ate breakfast and when Miquita's mother offers us something, we ask for water and she gives us milk. After which, Eleazar explains to her why we're here. Miquita seems to cringe at hearing this as if she's bothered by the reasoning behind my quest. To be honest, I'd be jealous too if I were in her position.

"That's great! Miquita here hasn't found her Heart Absolute ability either, but hopefully, she will someday."

"I hope so too so I can get out of this place. I'm tired of constantly doing farm work," Miquita comments.

"Farm work is humble, honest, and worthy of praise," Eleazar says.

"Sure."

"Heh, I think I know why we're here. Is it okay if we help you today?"

"Knock yourselves out."

Help her? Nothing about helping her sounds like the start of our previous adventures. Why is Eleazar looking at me as if he knows something I don't?

"What?" I say.

"Oh, nothing. You'll see why we're here soon enough."

"I hope so."

Eleazar gets changed into casual farm worker clothes that remind me of how he looked back when we were younger. For the whole day, we go from farm to farm helping people with their needs similar to what I do back home, which I hate. It's easy to get around thanks to

Eleazar's portals, but it still sucks. Why are we meant to do this? What am I meant to learn? This feels like a waste of time. Maybe I'll meet someone along the way who I'm actually meant to follow.

A little after noon, we eat lunch at one of the farms we work at. Eleazar is having fun chatting it up with the farmers inside so Miquita and I step outside since we aren't part of the conversation. While we're outside, she gives me a strange look that I catch before she can turn her head.

"What is it?" I ask.

"Nothing," she says.

"I know you looked at me."

"…That best friend of yours is annoying me. Can you tell him to stop being so positive and cheerful all the time?"

"Trust me, I've tried, but he never stops. Oh, and he's not my best friend. He just visits and bothers me from time and time, and this'll be my last time seeing him after I get my Heart Absolute ability."

"Heh, so you feel the same way I do about him. It must be nice being given this journey by the Absolute."

"It has its ups-and-downs. Still, even after witnessing so many big events, I don't completely understand what I'm supposed to learn."

"Even so, I wish I could go on an adventure like you. A girl like me probably won't see the world outside of this town for my entire life just like the other farmers and I don't think I'll ever get my Heart Absolute ability. All my efforts and prayers are for nothing as far as I'm concerned."

"I felt that way and still do to an extent."

"Tomorrow is my birthday. My parents invited everyone in the town that I've worked with, but I don't think anyone will come. These people don't really care about me. I'm just another farmer that does the job averagely well. I'll…I'm planning something that will either make my Heart Absolute ability or change my life for the better."

"How are those two things mutually exclusive?"

"Because…because I'm going to try to kill myself tomorrow."

"What?"

"I can't live like this anymore! You don't understand how hard it is living like this with people that don't appreciate you and people our age being put on pedestals because of their efforts or because they have their Heart Absolute ability."

"I understand completely as a community service worker who lives in pretty much the exact same situation."

"Community service worker? Heh, between that and that guy I understand why the Absolute had mercy on you and put you on your adventure. So, you must understand why I want to do what I'm going to do. If I try to kill myself, my Heart Absolute ability may kick in just like some of the stories I've heard. If I do end up dying, then at least I'll be free from this miserable life." Dang it. I don't feel like I could talk her out of this. "Thank you."

"For what?"

"For being here. It's good to know that there's at least one person who is like me in this world."

What am I going to do? Eleazar's positivity will probably make her want to kill herself more and I can't exactly argue with her without affirming her views. Perhaps the real person I'm supposed to follow will come to save her tomorrow? Tonight, Eleazar and I stay over at Miquita's house and sleep in the guest rooms. Unfortunately, I have to deal with Eleazar's snoring, which doesn't help me go to sleep when thoughts of Miquita's potential suicide attempt are already keeping me up. I spend the time I have awake praying that she doesn't do anything drastic or that her attempt fails at least.

Early in the morning, I wake up as soon as the rooster crows and try to find Miquita. I find her outside putting a noose around her neck and a rope around a wooden beam. Running outside, I try to find words to say, but just end up saying nothing except for her name.

"Hey. I'm glad that you're here at least," Miquita says.

"Hold on," I say.

"It's going to be okay. Let's see how those ungrateful people react when they see me hanging. Who am I kidding? They probably won't care for long. Still, here's hoping I get my Heart Absolute ability, but I don't have much hope in it."

Before I can run up to Miquita to stop her, people come out of her home and her mom calls out to her. Everyone that's here seems to be concerned about Miquita. They're all people we met yesterday and have presents in their hands. Seeing everyone makes Miquita take the noose off her neck and walk toward us. She's speechless and looks like she's about to cry as her parents embrace and berate her at the same time with tears in their eyes as well.

"I thought you didn't love me because I didn't have any unique abilities like the others and because I'm working a dead end job," Miquita says.

"Honey, we still care about you despite that. Everyone here cares about you. You've touched their hearts with all your dedication and hard work. If anything, that's your amazing ability."

People start coming forward presenting gifts to Miquita along with their testimony of her hard work and how much they appreciate her despite her being just another farmer. One of the people that give her a gift and their appreciation is a young man that's about our age. He gives her a crown that he made from the flowers on his farm and basically confesses his love for her. All this puts a smile on Miquita's face and seems to change her not too dissimilar to the others that I've met with Heart Absolute ability. Miquita's parents hug me and thank me for saving her to which I can't say much since I didn't really do anything except stall her for a second.

Of course, because of this, I have to stay for Miquita's birthday celebration, and when everything is over, I'm left speechless to see nothing else happening. No one special comes and nothing spectacular really happens. While sitting on Miquita's porch waiting for something, anything else to happen, Eleazar sits next to me.

"You did something great today," he says.

"I didn't do anything special."

"You may think that, but it's you have to give yourself credit for saving Miquita."

"Whatever. I'm still waiting for the reason we came here."

"What are you talking about? We already accomplished it."

"I have no clue what you're talking about. I haven't learned anything new. What was I supposed to learn exactly? That sometimes we already have everything we need around us?"

"Exactly."

I can feel my heart stop for a second as soon as Eleazar said that. His smile fills me with such hatred for him that crushing his head passes my mind for a second.

"No, no! Take me somewhere else!"

"There's no point in it. I might as well take you home. I'm sure your parents are worried about you-"

"No, they're not! They don't care about me!"

"Miquita thought the same and looked at what happened with her."

"I'm different though. Take me back to your advisor and ask him if there's anything else we need to do."

"Let me see if the Absolute will let me."

A portal opens up and brings us to the office with Adivino at the front desk like he was before.

"Ah! Eleazar and Cornelia! How did your adventures go?" he asks.

"Tell me there's something else I have to do. Tell me I missed something," I say.

"For what reason?"

"I don't have my Heart Absolute ability. Nothing has changed about me and I haven't learned anything."

Adivino looks confused and then at Eleazar who shrugs.

"Okay. If you've gone through everything you were supposed to, this shouldn't take too long."

I pace around waiting and thinking about what I could've possibly missed for a short while before Adivino comes back to confirm that there's nothing more that I need to do and I already have everything I need. This upsets me to no end and I almost scream out loud.

"See? I was right," Eleazar says.

"Shut up!" I snap at him.

"Hey, calm down. It's okay to accept things the way they are."

"I refuse to accept that I went on that adventure for nothing!"

"You didn't go on it for nothing. We learned about what being conceited does to a person and how the Absolute can save the conceited through an unlikely person with Lionel. From Caleb and Kyla, we learned that having a Heart Absolute ability doesn't instantly make your life better, happy, or make you perfect. Finally, with Miquita, we learned that a person's Heart Absolute ability doesn't have to be something grand or magical, it isn't always obvious, and that even the simplest Heart Absolute abilities are greatly appreciated and needed all the same."

What Eleazar says hurts my ears to hear them because I realized the same things but didn't want to accept them. Still…still…there could be a chance.

"Take me somewhere else."

"I can't take you anywhere the Absolute doesn't want me to. If the Absolute wants you to go home, you'll go home."

"But if I'm supposed to go somewhere else, we'll go somewhere else. Prove me wrong that I'm meant to go home."

"Okay."

Eleazar opens a portal to a place that blinds me with its light. Hopefully, this isn't home. Come on! Prove me right! This can't be the end of my journey!

Chapter 5 – Having Heart vs Being Heartless

The light from around us subsides as my eyes get used to it. Eleazar and I find ourselves on a mountain that seems like an elaborate marketplace with different kinds of vendors ranging from farmers to blacksmiths to butchers. For some reason, there are also helpers that travel on carts from place to place to help with whatever the vendor needs from cleaning their storefront or transporting their goods from one place to another on the mountain.

"What is this place?" I ask.

"This is an amazing place for you to start anew and make the most of your Heart Absolute ability," Eleazar says.

"What are you talking about?"

"This mountain is a place many people gather such as community service workers to either get noticed or work in this center of trade in this region. Many people across this land come here for trade and the shelter that the people that live on this humongous mountain provide. I'll tell your parents that you're here and get what you need to start off strong here. I'm sure they'll accept you when you get a recommendation from my office."

It can't be…

"No, no, no!"

Looking around, I find the blacksmith and run towards it.

"Where are you going? What's wrong?" Eleazar says while following me.

"Shut up and stop following me! Stay away!"

Entering the blacksmith's shop, I leap over the tables, grab a sword, and am about to fall on it until the blacksmith stops me along with his other workers in the shop. They try to tell me to stop and the reasons why I shouldn't take my own life, but I don't listen as I fight them off and try to keep stabbing myself. Eleazar enters the shop and is the one to take away the sword while the blacksmith and his workers restrain me.

"What's wrong with you, Cornelia?" Eleazar asks me.

"Shut up! You don't understand! I don't want to live this life!" I say.

"Why not? It's meaningful and honorable. It's a life you're meant to live. This is what you've been waiting for where you can truly become who you're meant to be!"

"No, it isn't! You don't know me at all."

"I'm your best friend. Of course I-"

"No, you aren't! I hate you! I hate everything about you and you never shut up enough to realize it!"

Something in Eleazar's expression seems to finally listen to me.

"…you don't mean that."

"I do! I hate you! I hate my parents, I hate all the people I've worked for, and I hate the Absolute for wasting my time! I can't believe that it put me on this journey with you just for a reminder. I won't believe it. I refuse to! If the Absolute won't give me what's due to me, then I'll take it for myself."

As I'm saying all of this, I haven't noticed my body changing. My entire body is now naked and white with a large heart shaped hole in my chest with a black heart floating in the center. In addition, one of my arms and both of my legs are now black. The only thing that hasn't changed as much is my one arm that has my bracelets on them and even this has changed with my middle finger being white and blade-like now. This appearance has scared away the blacksmith and his workers who have grabbed their nearby weapons and surround me.

"Cornelia, listen to me," Eleazar says.

"No, you listen to me now," I say while holding out my black arm.

Black energy emanates from my black arm and I can feel it touch the hearts of everyone around me. Through this new power of mine, I can feel their doubts, fears, and wants to do something else than what they are doing. Taking advantage of this, I bend their will to listen to me except for Eleazar who is resistant. The blacksmith and his workers are now behind me and face down Eleazar who is backing away and out of the shop.

"Cornelia…you have to stop," he says with an arm out.

"Stop? I like this new ability of mine. It's not exactly what I thought I wanted, but it meets my needs and I'm keeping it," I say.

"You're being conceited. You're not being yourself. This power isn't you."

"And who are you to define that? I will define myself."

"You can't do that. Only the Absolute knows who you truly are."

"I don't care about the Absolute anymore. It never cared about me, to begin with." I pick up Eleazar by the neck and squeeze his neck. "If you trust the Absolute so much, then surely you will be saved."

I then throw Eleazar down the mountain seeing him violently hit the large rocks on the way down. Looks like the Absolute deemed you not worth saving. I don't see his body now that it's fallen far away and into some bushes and tall grass, but even if he ends up teleporting and coming back, I won't mind killing him with my own hands. Everyone around me starts staring and getting their weapons, runs, or hides in fear. With my new ability, I take control of their hearts and find that my control can spread from person to person when they come into contact with one another and the more people under my control that surround a person, the easier it is to take control of their hearts. Many are now under my control with very few managing to get away since I sense their pain and take advantage of it. It makes sense because of the jobs they have and all the pain they go through and get little to no respect in return. My life's goal has now been revealed to me.

"Together, we will free the world from the chains of hard labor and get our just rewards!" I say, "It is said that the Absolute knows you best, but who really knows you better than yourself? Is this fate of working till your death really the best? I don't think so. We will spread the good news of being conceited as the better option and free people from the chains of the Absolute!"

Everyone around me cheers and some of them even begin to look like me with heart shaped holes in their chest though they also grow black crowns on their head. They start gathering their weapons and horses as we mobilize for war and the spreading of our truth. When one of my supporters comes close to me with a shield, I take a better look at myself and see that one of my eyes is completely grey, I have black wings on my back, and parts of my hair have blackened and raised to form a pseudo crown. Yes, I think this look suits me. I grab a map and plot my army's course to a nearby settlement where we can get more people. Once everyone is together, I fly to the front at the bottom of the mountain.

"Forward! I, Cornelia Queen of the Commoners, will lead us to victory. We will finally take what is rightfully ours!" I say to the cheers of my soldiers.

War, Love, and the Absolute

We mobilize and hit our first destination not long after. At the settlement, we take what we want and influence more people to join us even if they resist. Having so many hearts under my control feels unnatural and wonderful at the same time. Their pain is mine and mine is theirs. I feel what they do and we understand each other. When we're ready with more turning conceited, we move to our next location. Since I'm feeling good, I pick a city not too far from here to go to since I want the Church to pay for its teachings.

Along the way to the city, we come across outposts and smaller settlements that we take control of and rest at when needed. With more people, the stronger I feel and the stronger they feel, the stronger I get. Our numbers grow and grow until I feel that taking the city will be easy even when I overlook it. This city looks like a lot of the other major cities with heart shaped designs on the major buildings and Churches. Surely, this will be a good place to be the home of my new kingdom. Once I take it, more people will become conceited and see that it's superior to the Heart Absolute abilities. I have so many soldiers and supporters behind me that I choose to send all of them to the city at the same time to surround it from all angles before going into it.

The assault goes well until we reach the innermost walls of the city where my army fights against many who have Heart Absolute abilities. For the past day, those with Heart Absolute abilities can be overwhelmed with numbers, but this many can be a problem. It's no real issue. There are more people in this city that are hiding that I can use to add to my forces. While doing this, I come across a young girl who walks out of the dark. She wears simple teal robes and brown boots.

"Have you come to challenge me or join my army?" I ask her.

"Neither because you will challenge a servile," she says.

"You can summon serviles? How unique of you at such a young age to have a Heart Absolute ability like that. What makes you think one will come to save you when the Absolute has abandoned your city?"

"We are not abandoned. Face your own guardian servile."

Time looks to be stopped all already me. I try to use my abilities, but nothing happens. My wings don't even allow me to fly anymore.

"Cease your sin," a voice says from behind me.

Turning around, I see a being made of equipment that I've used such as dusters, garden forks, and even dirty hands. Some of these objects also comprise its wings.

"Or what?" I say to it.

"You will be lost forever."

"I will not! I'll be remembered forever!"

With one of my black arms, I try influencing the servile only for it to shatter. After this, I try my legs and then my wings all of which shatter leaving me with nothing but my arm that still has my bracelets on them. Even with this, my attacks don't affect the servile though I still try to fight it.

"This won't accomplish anything," the servile says.

"I don't care! I'll make something happen with my own will!" I say.

"Can you make the water feel dry? Can you make fire feel wet? Can you make the darkness brighten up the sun? You cannot do something that is false."

"I got this power without the Absolute's help. I can do anything I put my heart to!"

"You were only allowed your abilities because the Absolute allowed it and it is only an inverse of your Heart Absolute ability. Instead of being able to serve many, you now make others serve you."

"That's right because I deserve it after suffering so much in life. The only thing I was ever given for my efforts were these bracelets, which the Absolute had no part in."

"False again. You were given those bracelets and allowed to keep them because it was one of the times you went out of your way to help someone without thinking about a reward. Look at how this arm of yours is the only thing that's living. It's supposed to remind you of the humility that's truly you."

"Don't talk to me as if you know me better than myself."

"Then think about others. You can feel their emotions and their pain. Do you think they're happy like this? Don't you feel the same dead chill that inhabits their bodies and yours?"

I do feel it. Focusing on it makes me feel it more intensely for some reason. A pain that goes beyond their want to be repaid for their efforts. I feel their hearts yearning for something else. They yearn to be true. It's a feeling that their hearts have and mine.

"Okay, okay. I see your point. You have your victory over me. Finish me off and end my sinful life."

"I am not your executioner. I am your guardian servile. My victory is achieved when the Absolute's will is done. This includes your redemption and salvation."

"I'm sorry then. I'm sorry for everything I've done. I've been so selfish that I didn't realize of all the people I've hurt and the love I've shunned."

"Rise then and become who you truly are, Cornelia."

My appearance changes back to normal though it doesn't seem to be as normal since my hair looks a lighter brown and I feel lighter too. My connection to the others has ceased and it gets quiet in the city after a few seconds. The girl who showed me my guardian servile gives me brown rags to clothe my nakedness and then hugs me.

"I know what it's like to lose yourself. I'm glad that you came back to your senses," the girl says.

"Thank you," I say while holding back my tears, "I don't know how to thank you."

"You should leave before the guards come. Go back home. There should be horses you can use near the gates of the city."

"Thank you again. I'll try to repay you someday."

"You don't have to. Seeing you back to normal is enough for me now go."

I hurry, find a horse, and use the map I have to go back home. It takes me half a day of traveling, but when I get back home early in the morning, I'm hesitant to approach my house and think about leaving. That is until I see them at the window before coming outside. They call out my name and I get off the horse and meekly walk to them with my head down expecting to be scolded. Instead, they embrace me while crying and saying how much they miss me.

"I'm sorry for wasting so much time. I had my Heart Absolute ability all along. Heh, it's tacky I know. I'm sorry that I can't be anything else than a community service worker," I say.

"That's fine! You always were a hard worker that had the admiration of the people who apricated your work," my mother says.

"There's no shame in your work, Cornelia. You only needed to put your heart into it, which is something that I always told you to do. Regardless, let's get you inside and something to eat and you can tell us all about your adventures. Where's Eleazar by the way?" my father says.

"Umm. That's going to take a lot to explain."

After going inside and eating a bit, I tell my parents everything that happened including what I did to Eleazar and what I did while conceited. Even though they are concerned, they are happy that I came to my senses and learned my lesson, which I'm surprised by.

"Next time you feel that no one is appreciating you, talk to us. We're your parents and supposed to listen and care for you. I'm sorry we caused you so much grief," my mother says.

"I'm sorry for doing the same to you," I confess.

Speaking about confessions, I go to confession after eating and the priest has the same reaction my parents had and says similar things.

"You're a good person, Cornelia. No matter what happens, remember the love of the Absolute, the love of your family, the love of the neighbors around you, and you'll never lose yourself again," the priest adds as advice after giving me my penance.

Despite this being advice that I know, past events have shown that I need to be constantly reminded of the basics, so I thank the priest for it. For the next couple of days, I try to appreciate them as best I can. I even dress differently by wearing lighter colors, wearing a brown dress, a white apron, and light brown boots. In addition, I also tie my hair up for a different look. To be honest, the change of thinking every day as a gift and recognizing the small, good things in life that the Absolute gives makes a big difference. Work is actually bearable now, I appreciate the compliments and little gifts that the people I work with give me, and I hardly feel bitter.

Everything seems to be getting better for me until soldiers from the Kingdom of Simbiosi come strolling into town with Caleb and Kyla leading them. Oh yeah. I probably wasn't going to get away with what I did because I said I was sorry and did penance. I hear them calling my name and present myself to them without resisting arrest.

"For your sentence, you will be serving as a house cleaner for our castle for ten years," Kyla says.

"Really?" I ask in surprise expecting something worse.

"Shush. Do you know how hard it was to lessen your sentence? It's thanks to us knowing you plus your boyfriend's help that you're getting off easy," Caleb says.

"Boyfriend?" A face I thought I would never see again comes out of the crowd of soldiers on horseback. It's Eleazar! He's all banged up, one of his arms is broken, and his face is scarred, but he's alive! "Eleazar! I'm…I'm sorry for what I did to you and-"

"I know you're sorry, and don't worry about it. I'm just glad you're back to being truly yourself," he says with a smile.

I'm about to be put in a prison cart before I hear my name being called out. Turning around, I see the boy who made me the bracelets I wear every day.

"What? You have another boyfriend?" Caleb says.

"Oh, shut up. This is the boy that made these bracelets for me. Can I talk to him before I go?" I ask.

"Sure thing," Kyla says.

Going to the boy, I see him holding a crown made of flowers in his hands.

He's shy to talk to me at first until he holds up the crown and says, "I've wanted to give this to you for a while, but was never brave enough to do so and since you're going away for a while, I thought I'd give it you now."

"Thank you so much. I love it just like my bracelets."

I bend my head down and the boy puts the crown of flowers on my head. Since his head is close, I give him a kiss on the forehead as thanks, which makes his face turn red.

"Umm. Thank you too." Before I go, I hear the boy running after me again. "Excuse me! Can I go with her? I'll serve my own sentence as long as I get to be with her."

"You haven't done anything wrong," Caleb says.

The boy runs up to Eleazar and hits him in his injured arm, which I can't help but laugh at.

"There! I assaulted someone. That deserves some kind of punishment."

"Okay, okay! Get inside the cart with your girlfriend."

"I wish you were that bold," Kyla says to Caleb.

"When am I not?!"

When he's let in the cart, I give the boy a hug and another kiss to which he blushes again. He says goodbye to his parents who are somewhat upset, to say the least at him. Honestly, I didn't expect my life to be this way and what I wanted, but it is. I guess the Absolute really does know people better than they know themselves. I'm truly happy for the first time in a while and smile and look out at the

sun as I await a bright future.

The End

War, Love, and the Absolute

- Originally, chapter 4 was going to be about Cornelia witnessing two people who are like Miquita except one would be more positive while the other would be more negative. They would've fought and Cornelia would've had to reconcile them. I changed this because I thought one character being like Cornelia and the events that happened in chapter 4 were a better choice to reflect herself and her thoughts.

- This series is mostly inspired by the *Kingdom Hearts* series by Square Enix and Disney.

- The secondary inspiration for this series are the *Disney* princess movies and fairy tales such as those by the *Brothers Grimm*.

- Cornelia is one of my favorite characters that I've made. What I relate to the most is her bitterness, which I felt a lot of while writing her story.

- Just like Cornelia, I wear bracelets that were given to me and make me feel appreciated except I didn't mean to reference it in the story. These skull bracelets that I have were given to me by a co-worker, Mr. John, as thanks for giving him a signed copy of one of my books.

Cover made by @An_dres_art (on Twitter)

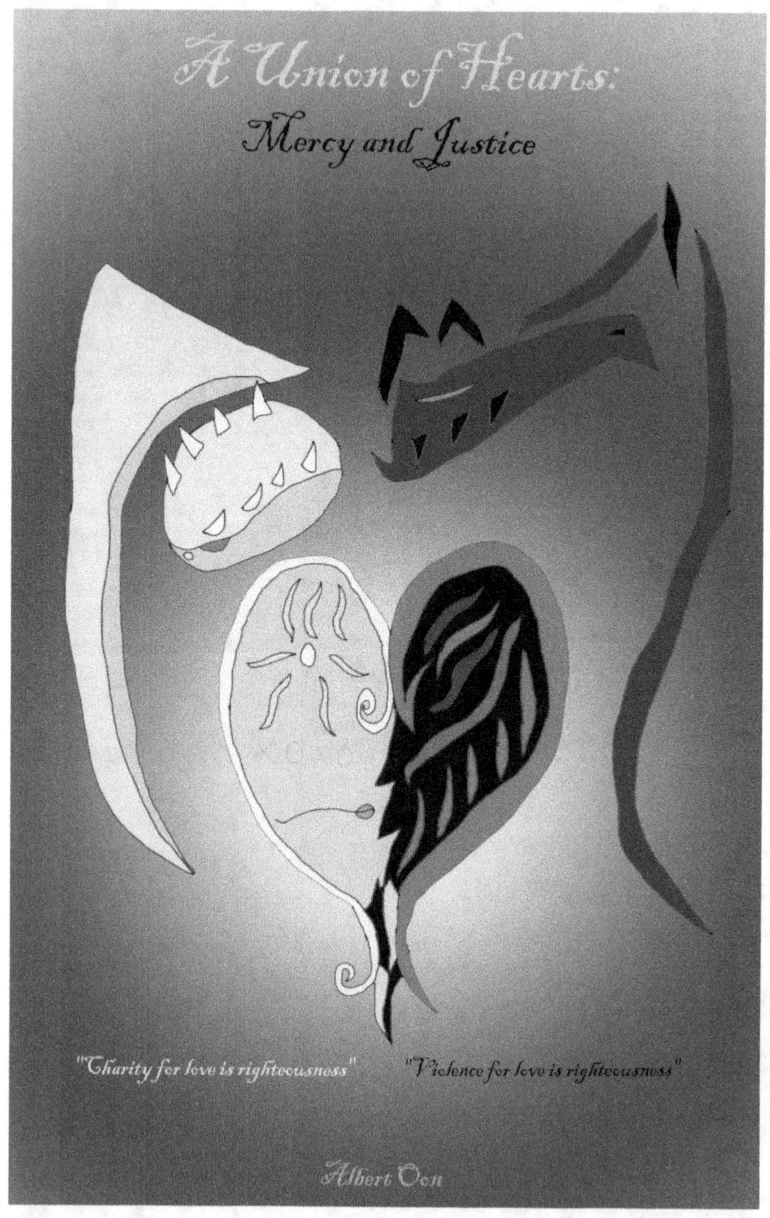

The original cover for this story made by Albert Oon.

*Concept art for Caleb and Kyla

Chapter 1 – A War of Love against Love

A loud noise wakes Kyla and me from our sleep.

"We're under attack!" a servant says as they barrage into our room.

"Yeah, we know! Get everyone to safety!" I say.

Kyla and I dress in our armor and get our weapons before heading upstairs as fast as we can. Looking out the windows, we see that what look to be black and white cannon balls are hitting our castle and the surrounding city.

One of these volleys tears open the wall in front of us giving us a convenient way out. We jump out of this hole and onto our dragons that materialize below us. My dragon fires volleys of crimson flame while Kyla's dragon fires volleys of blue flame to intercept the ones coming at us and into the city.

On the ground, we can see black and white creatures without heads and have blades and shields for limbs some of which are no bigger than an infant and have blades for heads. All of these creatures come in the same way as volleys by flying over the wall and taking their shape when they hit the ground before moving to attack everyone in sight that isn't like them. Kyla and I command our dragons to continue to intercept the incoming enemies while we go on the ground to attack the black and white creatures. Once our army and city's guards get a hold of the situation, we go back in the air. Our citizens, the soldiers, and the guards cheer for us as we fly over them.

"I didn't expect Absalom to make his move against us so early," Kyla says.

"What else were you expecting from a man whose influence is quickly spreading throughout the world?" I ask.

"Some restraint so you don't turn everyone against you?"

"Not Absalom. It's not like him when he has his heart set on something, especially with his new family and conceited powers."

Beyond the walls is a small army of black and white creatures and conceited people with heart shaped black holes in their chests. Our dragons rain down their fire on this army that creates a tornado of crimson and blue fire, and in minutes, this army is brought to its knees or reduced to ashes based on the mercy and justice of the Absolute. We bring back those that are still alive for questioning and are cheered for on the way back into the city. While we wait to hear the results of the interrogation, we help the citizens and guards clean up the mess the attackers made.

"Absalom has finally given us the reason we need to go after him ourselves," I say.

"Still, it's not like him to attack us like this," Kyla says.

"He's conceited, which means he'll go from sin to sin and he's no longer himself. That means he'll be unpredictable from now on."

"He is unpredictable but part of him must still be alive since he still lives. The Absolute doesn't make anyone live forever in falsehood."

"We can only hope that's the case," we hear a man say from behind us.

A general from our army approaches us and we drop what we're doing to bow to him, greet him, and then shake his hand.

"What did you hear from the prisoners?" I ask.

"They told me that Absalom ordered the attack on our home through his specters, those black and white creatures that you saw," the general explains.

"I didn't know he could make so many with his conceited heart," Kyla says.

"They are weaker than the ones that he used to make when he was himself and had his Heart Absolute ability. I've already talked to the other leaders in the city and we think it's time we launched our own assault against him."

"It's about time that decision was made. When do Kyla and I leave?" I say.

"You leave after we make the decision official and receive a blessing from the archbishop. We still have to plan out how we're going to go about this attack. Your parents should have come back from their own missions with valuable information on the cities that have fallen under Absalom's influence, but they haven't yet. It's unlike them to be this late."

"We'll go after them as well. The places they were investigating are on the way to Absalom's main city."

"I wouldn't be too hasty about getting there. He did take over the entire city by himself after all."

"We also haven't perfected our own Heart Absolute ability, so going up against a veteran like him and his army of specters is going to be dangerous even with the power of our dragons of mercy and justice," Kyla adds.

"I'm not worried. If the situation gets sticky, we'll combine our dragons and hearts into one. That thing can destroy false gods."

"It also takes a lot out of us to use, so we can't abuse that power."

"Whatever you say."

"She's right, Caleb. Absalom fought in many more battles than the both of you combined. Don't underestimate him just because he's conceited. You too may have your Heart Absolute ability and it may be one of the best out there but remember it doesn't make you perfect nor unbeatable."

"Okay, I won't. You don't need to remind me of a lesson I already learned."

After finishing helping the citizens clean up, we go back home to our castle to eat and prepare for our deployment. Our table is already set with our servants eating before us. It's a rule that they do not wait for us if we're late. Many of them are concerned about what happened and we fill them in.

"Well, get as much rest as you can before you head out," one of our servants says.

"Yeah, and you better enjoy this breakfast that Cornelia helped make. She worked really hard on it like she always does," her boyfriend says.

"It is but, it won't cut time off her sentence so you can stop mentioning how hard she works," I say.

Cornelia's boyfriend hits me on the shoulder and then says, "Hey! She better get something extra for all the extra work she does for you!"

"It's okay, Stallworth. Don't worry about it," Cornelia says.

It's a tradition in our kingdom to allow repentant criminals to be our servants to serve out their sentence whereas before they became slaves for the rest of their lives. Cornelia is one of these criminals who was taking over parts of our kingdom, but she repented of her sins and gave herself up to us when we came for her. It also helped that we met previously and her friend picked up for her. Her boyfriend, Stallworth, isn't a criminal at all and just came with her because she loves her. We allow this because of their love and the two serve us along with other servants who were once criminals and conceited.

War, Love, and the Absolute

Stallworth is still staring at me as if he's trying to intimidate me into giving his girlfriend something extra as thanks for her efforts as if we haven't done that and still do that today. The guy is younger and smaller than us, and yet, he has the presence and determination of a man twice his size. When he asked me to train him, I kept knocking him down and he kept getting up no matter how many times and how hard he got hit. If he has his Heart Absolute ability, his ability probably gives him resilience. He's also asked me how I proposed to Kyla so he can have an idea as to how to propose to Cornelia and even asked for extra work so he can earn a ring to give to her one day. I gave him one of the best rings we have in our jewelry collection. It's not like we wear all of them anyway.

He was astonished I did this and really should remember it not as extra thanks or payment for his work and the work of his girlfriend, but to remember that we do things out of kindness in the Kingdom of Simbiosi to replicate what the Absolute does for us. I wonder when he'll propose. It has been a month since Cornelia and Stallworth started their relationship, so it should be soon. Kyla and I were married after a month and a half of knowing each other. I'm sure that Kyla wants to see the two married. She still admires Stallworth for offering his freedom up so that he could be a servant in this castle with Cornelia. What I find most impressive about him is not his tenacity, but the crown of flowers that he made for Cornelia that she wears every day in addition to the colorful bracelets he also made. The flowers haven't rotted or changed and still smell fresh. Even though Cornelia isn't royalty like Kyla or me, she's allowed to wear her crown since the Absolute crowned her through Stallworth because of her conversion, and who are we to take away the crown of someone who rightfully deserves it? We might as well give up our own crowns if that's the case.

War, Love, and the Absolute

After breakfast, Kyla and I clean ourselves up

before heading out. I wear a traditional crimson and black

set of armor that has spikes on its shoulders and arms. In

addition, I wear a helm that has spikes on it like the spiked

crown of my dragon. Kyla wears her crown of gold and

blue stones and a silky silver and light battle dress, which is

decent protection and allows her to move swiftly in battle

like a rose petal through the air. I've tried suggesting that

she wear something like I do, but she always denies it since

she prefers outfits that originate from her side of the

kingdom. To be honest, I don't care what she wears because

she looks beautiful in everything. Her captivating gold hair

and gold and silver eyes never cease to capture my eyes.

She says the same about my gold and black eyes and my

crimson-colored shaved head.

We then go to the grand cathedral, which never

ceases to amaze me, especially with its dual design that

shows both sides of Simbiosi. Both sides of the cathedral

have statues of serviles, who are angels and loyal servants of the Absolute. One side has these serviles holding books and shields while the serviles on the other side hold swords and scales. Further inside the cathedral are statues and paintings of heroes and depictions of historical and scriptural events. Our kingdom gathers and separates itself based on which side they're from as the ceremony begins. Eventually, we go up to the altar where we kneel before the archbishop who holds out his hands over us.

"Prince Caleb and Princess Kyla, receive this blessing of the Absolute through me to aid you in your future battles not only in the physical sense but also the spiritual and moral. Deliver mercy to our enemies so that they may know the Absolute's love, be saved, and be welcomed in the Land of the True. Deliver justice to our enemies so that they may know the Absolute's love, shorten their sinful lives, and be condemned to the Land of the Forgotten. Whether mercy or justice, deliver the

Absolute's love to our enemies in all its forms either in charity or violence. This the Absolute commands and blesses you in doing this holy work. Bring them all to Divine Judgment, be pure of heart, and yourselves as you were made to be as you will be judged as all sinners are judged," the archbishop says.

Kyla and I say together, "We accept our duty and give our lives to truth and love."

The archbishop gives us our blessing and the ceremony ends. Once this is done, a mass is held and then we head out on our dragons to the cheers of our people that pray for our success. I kind of wish our friend who could teleport us around was here, but because of what Cornelia did to him, he's still resting at home. Regardless, Kyla and I start our war against Absalom to bring an end to his corrupting influence and to save not only our parents and our kingdom but also the world at large.

*Concept art for the dragons of mercy (left) and justice (right)

Chapter 2 – Knowing Your Enemy

After flying for a while, I see that Caleb has fallen seemingly asleep on his dragon.

"Shouldn't you stay awake just in case we're ambushed along the way?" I ask.

"I'd like an ambush right about now. You know I hate nothing more than doing nothing. Besides, my dragon will wake me up if there is a surprise attack," Caleb says.

Tch. Caleb can never enjoy relaxation outside of sparring, sports, working out, and sleep. He never really does like traveling or going places just to admire their beauty. I guess I can't blame him too much because of the culture he was born into. Looking below us, I see the simple rolling hills and forests that always amaze me with their natural beauty.

"After we bring Absalom to judgment, we should go camping again," I suggest.

"Sure, it'll be a good excuse for getting out of politics," he nonchalantly says.

"If we do have to deal with political matters when we get back, then our rest will have to wait."

"Nah, we can let your side of the family handle it. I'd rather rake my brain trying to make poetry with you in the forest than deal with the politics of kingdoms and the Church."

"Then I'll make you sing and dance to those poems if that's really what you prefer."

"Sure, I accept that over politics."

If it doesn't have to deal with duty or politics, Caleb doesn't care. The part of the kingdom he's from leaves politics to my side, however, they are very duty bound and if something needs to be done, then they do it in one way with no questions asked and everything else becomes secondary. My side of the kingdom does value duty, but it also questions the way to accomplish it with mercy and justice being the obvious example. Also, part of me wishes Caleb didn't always say "sure" to everything I suggest if there isn't anything else he thinks is important that needs to be done.

"Promise me that the next time our appearance is mandatory at the next meetings you won't just skim over the information and make me make the decision for us?"

"I promise that all the information that doesn't interest me won't stick to my brain."

"You know politics can be interesting to be in."

"Liar."

"I'm not. It's like a game of chess and there are better ways to play it than just letting my side of the kingdom and me make all the decisions."

"But your side is the best at it. If my side or I tried our hand at it, then it wouldn't end so well as the history of our kingdom has shown. There's a reason why we're the duty bound soldiers and you're the big brained statescraftsmen. You aren't called the Wise Princess Kyla for nothing."

He's right and I can never argue around it so the conversation ends here. If only he could make arguments like this when we are making decisions for the kingdom, then he'd make a fine politician rather than just being a warrior prince. The only joy I find in this is his confidence and trust in the decisions I make, however, we are still the prince and princess of our kingdom and must make decisions together rather than him always saying "nah, you deal with it".

"Be alert! Our destination is close by," I say.

"Finally," Caleb says while stretching.

The city we're in is one from my side of the kingdom where my parents should be. Cities from my side are modeled after cities dreamt of in fairy tales and what future cities might look like when all evil and falsehood is erased from the world. Most of the buildings are a silvery or white color except for the churches which are light gold. When the color fades or is dirtied, the buildings are repainted or even given colorful designs based on the wants of the building's owners. People dance, make music, paint, erect statues, and write stories in the streets of the city as one creative force for the gain of each other and to proclaim the goodness and beauty of the Absolute.

War, Love, and the Absolute

As we land in the city, Caleb and I find it strange that no one comes to greet us or acknowledges our presence. My vision begins to blur and my hearing starts to become deaf. I reach out to Caleb, but he and everything around me disappears as all becomes black. My dragon is also gone and I can't summon it. It feels as if something is constricting my heart and abilities. Soon after, my body changes, and I become smaller and wear different clothes. The blackness disappears and presents a battle I remember being in. This was between a rebel city and Caleb and I were sent in to put an end to the violence. Unfortunately, it wasn't so cut and dry.

The enemy was prepared for us and had a few conceited people who could blow themselves up and they did when we had the advantage. Bodies from both sides liter the battlefield in front of the besieged city with my own body now being heavily injured as it remembers the situation I was in. A large force of enemies is coming in to finish off the wounded. Meanwhile, I feel that I am unable to move and may die any second now because of my wounds. It is then that Caleb, who is as injured as I am, stands in front of me. He can hardly manage to stand and even falls to his knees as he struggles to.

"Save yourself!" I say.

"What kind of husband leaves his wife to die alone?" he asks.

Now, he manages to stand, but he is quickly stabbed through the chest after only taking down a few of the conceited. I scream out and raise my hammers with the nonexistent strength in my body and kill a few of the conceited as well before a blade goes through my chest as well. Time slowly goes by as I feel a beating in my heart that defies my dying body. Blue flames engulf me and completely heal me while Caleb is engulfed in crimson flames and healed to full as well. Our dragons manifest themselves in these flames and burn all of the conceited around us to ash. This was the first time our Heart Absolute ability showed itself and the event seems to have temporarily broken the spell on us as everything turns to black again before putting Caleb and me into a castle that's decorated with designs of black hearts contrasted by white and gold walls, ceilings, and floors.

From one of these hearts comes a person cloaked in darkness, dressed in black, and crowned with a spiky black crown. Despite his appearance, I recognize him as Absalom. His face and body are scarred, a large heart-shaped hole is in his chest that exposes his shriveled black heart, and his once glowing green eyes that I've heard about are now a dark green and dark grey.

"Thanks for saving us the trouble of finding you, Absalom. You have a lot to answer for," Caleb says.

"You cannot harm me where we are. This is a dream after all," Absalom says.

"A dream?" I ask.

"Yes, a dream. One of my supporters from your kingdom has the ability to look through a person's memories and allow them to relive certain ones in a dream."

"I know who you're talking about but I can't remember his name."

"I don't blame you since not many do. They only know him for his ability and nothing more. He's a good man that got by on his job but wanted to do something more with his life to help people more than he could. Making people happy by allowing them to relive the past doesn't do much if anything for their present situation, so with the help of my specter that possesses him and gives him strength, I gave enhanced his Heart Absolute ability so that people can live through their memories and alter them with their minds to live the life they want. At the same time, their bodies go about taking care of themselves. He can also put people into dreams that are within a large vicinity around him. Even now, both of your bodies are resting or getting some food to eat or something to drink so that you stay alive outside of this dream."

"We can't control what we're dreaming. Where's our control? If this is a dream I can control, why aren't you dead yet?" Caleb asks.

"You can't kill a person in a dream and you have no control because my friend hasn't given you control. He's given control of your dreams to me instead because I want to look into your memories and I want to show you my own."

"We don't care about that. We've only come to bring you to judgment."

"Hmph. We'll see if you don't care by the end of it."

Again, Caleb and I are separated this time by a wall that comes out of the ground, and again, I am unable to summon my dragon. My body becomes younger and the castle around me turns into the castle I was raised in. I can see what Absalom is trying to learn about me. My brothers and sisters come out of their rooms dressed for the challenges they have to face.

"You'll lose this time, Kyla," one of them says.

"I'll be the princess of Simbiosi," another says.

"You aren't skilled enough for it. You should just let me represent the family."

This I remember too well. My siblings and I competed to be the representative of our family. They said a lot of mean things some of which they said to be competitive or to a joke. After that, we had to see if we would fall in love with someone from the other side of the kingdom. That's when I met Caleb. My surroundings and body change to reflect the change in the time period. I remember seeing Caleb training in a garden with training dummies. At the time, I was cautious to approach him not only because there are those in my kingdom that view the other side as single-minded soldiers who always resort to execution and violence, but also because I felt a connection in my heart to him. This type of feeling is from the Absolute that we met the person we were meant to be with.

Caleb seems to have felt this tug in his heart toward me as well. He turns around and is stunned to say anything at first. Every now and then, I get this sense from seeing him that feels like a taste of the Land of the True. A taste of Heaven. We look into each other's eyes for a time as we remember the first time seeing each other before turning back into our usual selves. The area shifts into a forest with Absalom sitting under a tree.

"Your story together seems romantic. Something that would be told in a fairy tale," Absalom says.

"Thanks, but I've had enough of this," Caleb says before taking his spear from his back and throwing it at Absalom.

The spear passes through Absalom and then appears back on Caleb's back. We see two boys fighting off a large pack of wolves.

"Run! I'll hold them off for you," the older brother says while pushing away the youngest.

At first, the youngest does what the oldest says but then runs back when he sees that the oldest is surrounded by wolves. The youngest runs back with his arm out for his brother and this is when white specters in the form of legless knights armed with swords, spears, and shields appear and fight off the wolves for the brothers.

"As you can see, the story behind my Heart Absolute ability isn't as story worthy as yours," Absalom says as the area around us shifts to what he tells us next. "Once I got my Heart Absolute ability, I tried to help as many people as I could and as a result, I attracted the attention of the Church and the royalty of the kingdom. Before I turned twenty, I fell in love and had a child."

Everything around us comes to a sudden stop as the setting is stuck in a burning town.

"I know this part of your life. Your family was killed by a rogue kingdom of the conceited," I say.

"That's right. There was barely enough of them to bury when I saw their bodies. The event still haunts me to this day as you can see in the specters I conjure. Some of them look like mangled bodies and limbless infants with blades for heads for this reason. My superiors said they would be protected and I had nothing to worry about, but that wasn't true. Even so, I directed my anger to the correct source and punished those who killed my family. After a couple of years, I was okay and blessed enough to have a new family…but…"

"They were killed as well even though they were protected by people close to you."

"…yes…"

This memory is drastically affecting him. He holds one of his cloaked arms over his face and we can hear cries all around us.

"Look, we know that it's sad what happened to your family, but it doesn't excuse what you're doing now," Caleb says.

"How does it not?" Absalom says as he collects himself, "I'm trying to create a better world through my army of specters."

"You're making people conceited and you've attacked our home and the homes of many others!"

"I have done no such thing."

"The people that you've killed would say otherwise."

"I gave strict orders to my allies and specters to not kill or harm anyone. The attack on your home was meant to be a show of force with damage only done to the city and not to its citizens."

"That's not what happened. You should know."

"I do know. I felt the pain of every specter that you strike down though you cannot kill me by killing them as you can see. What is this? I can see in your memories that you're telling the truth. Something's wrong with this. What is it?"

Absalom seems genuinely confused and distressed at what we're telling him as he paces back and forth while whispering to himself.

"Even if you didn't attack anyone, it's still wrong to convince people to be as conceited as you. You damn their souls to the Land of the Forgotten when you make them sin and lose themselves."

"The Absolute makes use of the conceited to bring about greater things. Even those who have their Heart Absolute abilities, fall to sin every once in a while, no matter how dedicated they are to being true to their real selves. With my conceited ability, I am no longer constricted to the number of specters I can conjure and I can empower the abilities of my allies with them. My Heart Absolute ability is nothing in comparison to what I can do now. Once my influence spreads throughout the word, I can empower the weak, defend the innocent at a moment's notice, cease all conflict by force, and give my new family and all families the peaceful world they deserve."

"I don't believe your plan will work," I say.

"Nothing good can come from those who are conceited and refuse to change," Caleb adds.

"If I don't do what I need to, then the world will continue to be engulfed in wars and violence. You won't even need to fight anymore in the world I'll create. You'll only need to govern and enjoy it. How does this world of peace not seem like one the Absolute wills to create?"

"We already told you that you will damn souls despite your best intentions," I say.

War, Love, and the Absolute

Something seems to have taken Absalom's attention

away from us.

"Then we'll have to agree to disagree for now. Your

parents are breaking through their dream, Kyla. This will

wake up everyone else as a result and you'll have to deal

with my allies who will defend themselves if you attack

them. Also, be careful with your citizens. You did wake

them up from the best dream they've had in a while."

The dream around Caleb and I fades away and we

find ourselves back in the city with people waking up and

wondering why they stopped dreaming. An explosion

catches everyone's attention. In the distance we see my

parents fighting people in the air. My parents can manifest

see-through parts of the dragon of mercy on their bodies

such as the wings, head, and legs to help them in battle. It's

their Heart Absolute ability that they use more for seeing if

a person is innocent and transportation than combat. Caleb

and I jump on our dragons and aid them in the air. As we

get closer, I see that the people that my parents are fighting have Absalom's specters help them fly as if they were puppets.

"Mother, father! We're here to help!" I say to them as we join the fight.

"Glad to see you're here, my daughter," my mother says.

"Let's finish this fight together then give them their trial assuming that our flames don't burn them to ash," my father says.

Together, my parents, Caleb, and I defeat the few conceited and the small squadron of specters they have as a backup and bring those that survive to the court square where people are publicly judged in front of the city. Some in the city are mad that they were taken out of the dream and the guards in the city have to make sure a riot isn't started. Others are mad that what they were seeing was a dream and want Absalom's supporters put to death, and finally, there are citizens who are not sure what is and what isn't real because of how long they were dreaming or because they were so engrossed in the dreams.

"Put us in prison or kill us and stop wasting our time," one of the conceited says.

"You deserve the honor of a trial as is the tradition of our people," my father says.

Caleb rolls his eyes and obviously wants to get this done as fast as the conceited do. Regardless, the conceited are allowed to defend their actions to receive a lesser sentence.

"We did what our hearts told us to do because we could no longer deal with the reality of this world that is constantly at war and filled with violence and tragedy. Absalom has the best solutions that the Church and the many kingdoms of the world lack. He will be our king, army, and guard all in one man. Though he makes us conceited and he is conceited, he is the closest thing to having the Absolute in the flesh today," one of the conceited says.

The other conceited say the same things in different ways and add in their praise for Absalom and how he helped them. My parents and Caleb give their judgments of them and decide their fate. What am I even going to say? My parents say they should be put in jail for five years and must work community service that fits their particular abilities until they repent. On the other hand, Caleb says that they should be put to work and jail until their deaths or they repent as is the usual sentence of this magnitude from his side of the kingdom. His side used to enslave their prisoners if they didn't kill them decades ago before our two sides of the kingdom came together.

Should I have them executed? There's a loud cry in the crowd for it and I'm feeling the urge to. These people were able to put this entire city in a dream. My parents were able to break it, but it took them a lot of time to do it.

Who knows if Absalom will send more specters here to strengthen them and put everyone in a deeper dream. Part of me also wants to spare them and agree with either my parents or Caleb. Even though they were spared from being turned to ash, this could be a test of my judgment. People who have been spared from the flames of mercy and justice don't always turn to ash if they deserve it. Caleb and I learned that the hard way and had to let go of our pride in our abilities so the flames could do what they needed to.

"Just say what your heart tells you," Caleb says as if he was reading my mind, "I know it's pure and wise enough to make the correct judgment."

At times like this, Caleb always seems to read my mind and say or do something to comfort me. Our hearts are connected so it shouldn't surprise me, but it always does. My parents smile and nod at me and seem to know how I'm feeling similarly to Caleb.

"It is my decision that these conceited should be jailed and put to work that suits their abilities until they repent of their evil deeds," I say to the mixed reception of the crowd around us. "All of us have been guilty of some sin and evil deed. Was there not a time when you were lost and obstinate in your sin and repented after a time? Were you not thankful that you were shown mercy rather than struck down in your shameful state when you weren't yourself? There was a time when I was in ignorance like that and I still am in some respects. That is why I have chosen to show mercy to these poor sinners and they will continue to receive it until the Absolute says otherwise."

The crowds now murmur among themselves until they start clapping and cheering my name.

"All hail the merciful and wise princess!" they chant.

"The princess has decided and it shall be so," my father says.

War, Love, and the Absolute

Looking back at Caleb, he winks at me with a smile and I wink back. After the prisoners are taken away and the public goes back to their daily business, Caleb and I take the time to talk to my parents before we go.

I hug them and then say, "It's good to see that you're safe. Do you need us to help you with anything before you go?"

"You've helped us plenty by being here," my mother says.

"Just be careful with Absalom. It took us a while to break through the dream his ally had on us. We'll be sure to keep that man under maximum security and no specter comes to possess him to give him his freighting power again. I can imagine that his other allies are just as powerful," my father says.

"We'll be careful. Still, Absalom confuses me. He said that his allies would attack us if we struck first, but they attacked you first, right?"

"Right. The specters inside of them tried to aid them in their fight so Absalom must've aided them."

"Why would he say what he said to us then? He also mentioned that he gave strict orders to his allies and specters not to attack anyone in our home, but that's exactly what they did. When we told him what happened and he saw it in our memories, he seemed distressed and confused."

"Who knows what's really going on in that madmen's head?" Caleb says.

"It's possible that he's being corrupted by the vainglory. Demons could be possessing his mind and then make him think he's innocent right after. He did use a dark ritual to gain his new power after all," my father suggests.

"That's probably the most likely scenario. We'll see what happens when we see Caleb's parents."

"Oh, I'm sure they'll be okay. I don't know a family tougher than them from their side of the kingdom."

"Thank you, sir. I have to say the same about your family as well with Kyla here being the toughest among you," Caleb says.

"That she is. Have you managed to beat her in sparing yet?"

"Of course I have."

"That's not what I heard."

"No, you heard the victories I gave her."

"What are you talking about? I beat you fair and square a few times," I say.

"I don't want to see you cry because I'm constantly besting you, so I give you a victory every now and then."

"You're lying!"

"No, I'm not. I'm being honest."

"Fine then. When this is over, we'll spar until I beat you for real and I end up with more victories than you."

"Deal."

Albert Oon

Caleb and I say our goodbyes to my parents and then head off to see if his parents need him. I think we've learned a lot about our enemy and our weakness against him, but also what we can do. If my parents can break through Absalom's power, then so can we. With our hearts, our love, our strength, and the Absolute, we can accomplish anything after all.

*Concept art for Caleb and Kyla's combined dragon, the Judgment of the Absolute.

Chapter 3 - Honor Through Violence

"Caleb, are you falling asleep again?" Kyla asks me.

"I'm trying not to," I say.

Kyla and I took a nap and ate a bit at an inn before heading back out to check on my parents who are supposed to be investigating a city that's under the influence of Absalom. The short downtime has reminded me that we didn't learn anything useful about him when we met him.

Sure, we didn't know he could empower his allies with his specters, but that's not enough. We don't know the full extent of his power. What's obvious to me is that the vainglory are influencing him and we may have to deal with a demonic threat that's worse than the sorrowful wrath of a man who's been brought down by the tragedies of his life and the reality of this world.

From what we've heard from travelers at the inn, there's an eerie red fog where the city we're headed to is supposed to be, and those that dare head in the direction of the city are never heard from again. Not even our parents have come out nor any soldier or person with a Heart Absolute ability that can do anything. The neighboring towns and cities in the area have been careful in who they sent their messages to so that no one else will find themselves lost in the fog. This is clearly the work of Absalom and his ally must be the one responsible for the fog. When I heard of the fog, part of it reminded me of someone in the city, but I didn't know who so I kept quiet about it. Now, I think I remember.

"I think I know what's in the red fog," I say.

"What is it? Is it like the man who could put people in dreams?" Kyla asks.

"Sort of. It's similar to Absalom's power except it's more limited. I remember it being called the fog of war because it put individuals or groups of people into nonlethal battle scenarios for training."

"That's probably what we're going to be dealing with. How do you think we should approach it?"

"Head on."

"Seriously?"

"There's nothing we can do from the outside. What? Do you want to try to dispel fog with our flames or shoot fireballs into the city until we hit the user of the ability?"

"Fine. We'll go with your plan."

I'd honestly like to hear something better from Kyla, but since we're dealing with something mostly unknown, then we can only guess what to do. We continue traveling until we find the red fog that covers a large portion of the land. Heading in, we're surprised that we don't find any buildings around us. Instead, we find a forest as if a city was never built here. I look up and see that the red fog that we passed through is gone, which probably means that we're trapped in here until we can figure out what to do.

"This place is beautiful, isn't it," Absalom says as he appears from behind a tree.

Instantly, my dragon breathes its fire on him, however, only the trees around him are burned and catch fire.

"Why do you got to be so predictable? Why don't you face us in person?" I ask.

"Why do you have you resort to violence before I say anything?"

"Because you deserve it."

"I think it's because you were raised that way. Your side of the kingdom has always been prone to violence and kept on a short leash by the other side of it. Do you know of the time when both kingdoms were separate and had distinct names?"

"I remember from my history lessons. My side was called Vindicta and the other side was called Miserationem. They're both still called that by few people sometimes, but the distinction doesn't matter anymore since we're one people."

"I must admit that you're right on that part. Even the merciful side is prone to violence now. The kingdom of Simbiosi is one of the Church's peacekeepers and seemingly the biggest out of them and therefore guilty of the most bloodshed."

"We fight for those we love and bring justice to the wicked. What point are you trying to make? Get to it so I can fight you already and get to my parents."

"My point is to remind you that your kingdom, the Church, and the powers that be are one of the reasons the world is in a constant state of war and tragedy. Why don't you see that it needs to end sooner rather than later? With my solution rather than yours?" Scenes of some of the most intense battles and struggles pass us by. "Look at it all! Doesn't it sicken you? Don't you think about the many children that are orphaned, the people that are enslaved, and those that die horrible deaths for nothing?"

"I do think about it. How can I not when my entire life revolves around fighting? I think about the worth of every fight I get into and what may come of it as a result. I'm fighting against you because I know you're wrong and the people who have convinced me of my reasons to fight and live a life of war against evil are right."

War, Love, and the Absolute

"Don't you ever consider that they're wrong?"

"I have, but I trust the Absolute to guide my heart to make the right decisions and the Absolute is never wrong, and may the Absolute have mercy on me if I'm guided by my own foolish mind."

"What about your life of war? Do you really want to fight all of your life?"

"I'd rather not honestly. I want to make the world peaceful for those that I love and this includes getting rid of conceited people like you that will ruin it if you get your way."

"Kyla, are you going to let your husband do this? Don't you prefer mercy over violence?"

"I do, but mercy comes in the form of violence in this case. We will use it to punish you and your allies for your actions. Hopefully, your defeat will open your eyes and make you repent," Kyla says while taking out her hammers.

I take out my weapons as well and prepare to fight.

"I see. If you won't change your mind, then I have no choice but to defend myself and kill you and your supporters. You have your loved ones to fight and die for and so do I. When you lie dying in the dirt, remember that I gave you a chance to peacefully work this out."

The entire forest around us starts to burn around us as Absalom turns into a specter and then disappears. In the distance, we see two armies approaching on both sides. Both of these armies consist of Absalom's specters and his conceited allies, but one of them is led by a conceited man in armor and wielding a halberd. His armor is decorated with skulls and bones, and I'm sure he's the one controlling this since I know that the man with the ability to create war scenarios wears armor decorated with skulls and bones.

"Kill the warmongers!" the man in the armor says to his troops that scream in response.

War, Love, and the Absolute

Our dragons thin out the armies around us,

however, some manage to get through unscathed somehow.

Kyla and I fight on for a while until we realize that we may

soon be overwhelmed. The man decorated with bones is

down but not out as more specters continue to go into his

body to replenish his strength.

"We're going to have to use our combined power to

get through this," I say.

"I think so too. Are you ready?" Kyla says.

"Ready!"

Kyla and I hold each other's hands while our

dragons scream out and keep us safe.

"The two become one flesh. Let the Judgment of the

Absolute fall upon all of us!" we say together.

Our hearts, minds, and dragons are now one for the

time being as long as our strength holds out. The dragons of

mercy and justice are now one dragon called the Judgment

of the Absolute that has aspects of the dragons that

comprise it such as the shield-like wings of the dragon of mercy and the horns and thorny crown of the dragon of justice. Are you ready to finish this, Kyla? I'm ready, Caleb.

"Let the flames of mercy and justice come!" we say together.

In a gust of wind, our dragon flies into the air and sprays blue and red fire all around us that begins to clear the scenery around us that exposes the red fog and making it disappear. Soon enough, the red fog is gone. The city that is supposed to be here is revealed and everyone in it is freed. Sometimes, I wish more cities in the kingdom looked like this, Kyla. I prefer the ones that look like the city I'm from, Caleb. The whole spiky tops of the buildings and their dark colors of them give this oppressive feel to them. But they look so cool and give them so much personality that reflects our culture. I'm not saying they don't. We should look for your parents. They won't be too hard to look for. Look in the sky!

Above us, we see my parents flying around checking on everyone and probably looking for us. They have a similar Heart Absolute ability to your parents, Kyla. Yeah, except your parents manifest aspects of the dragon of justice instead of the dragon of mercy. Looks like they found us. They're coming down to us right now.

"Caleb! Kyla! We knew you had the power to break that spell," Caleb's father says while landing and the aspects of the dragon of justice disappear from him and his mother's body.

"We're sorry we couldn't break it ourselves," Caleb's mother says.

"There's no need to be sorry. We're glad to see that you're still alive and well," Caleb says.

"It's a good thing too because I sense an incoming battle."

"I sense it too. Are you two ready?"

"Yes, we are," we say together.

"Where's the enemy coming from?" Kyla asks.

"...all around us."

Caleb's parents and I fly up in the air with the aid of our dragon to see that the trees are coming to life. No, wait. The ones that are coming to life are specters of Absalom that were pretending to be trees. There are also conceited among them that were hiding in the surrounding forest. All of them are coming at us in full force so we must act quickly.

"Listen to me, people of Simbiosi!" Caleb's mother says in a voice that echoes throughout the entire city, "The conceited and vainglory are at our walls! Take up your arms! Defend your homes! Defend your loved ones! Fight for truth and love and all that is the Absolute!"

The entire city screams a battle roar as everyone who can take up arms does and since everyone who is from this side of the kingdom is given training in weapons, most if not everyone is ready to fight. They take weapons handed out to them by the blacksmiths, guards, and armies or take weapons from their homes and are then organized by Caleb's father who tells them where to go from the air. As for us, we hold hands again as our dragon breathes fire into the air to create a large ball of blue and red flames.

"O, loving and terrifying judgment of the Absolute, deliver your verdict!" we say as the fireball is complete.

The large ball of fire hangs in the air like the sun before one fireball of black and gold flames breaks it apart and spread it over the lands as far as the eye can see. We then join the fighting below and defeat the enemy army thanks to the help of Caleb's parents and the people of the city. After the fight, hardly anyone from the city is injured since the fire has been reported to heal them and turn to ash a majority of our enemies. In addition, the fire has also strangely not affected the forest. Instead, it has healed the wounds of battle inflicted on it and has seemingly made it more beautiful. Few of the conceited have survived and are sentenced without trial to a life of servitude and penance per the orders of Caleb's father. Our people celebrate this victory immediately when returning back to the city.

Caleb, we should join them and separate our dragons. I'm starting to get really tired of keeping it together. Me too, Kyla. It was fun and epic fighting like this together again. We'll probably have to do it again when fighting Absalom. Yeah, so let's rest as much as we can.

As we separate, our dragons separate too, and return to their original forms. A weight is also taken off my shoulders that was feeling a bit too much to bear, but I still feel my heart's connection to Kyla even though our minds aren't one. To be honest, I've felt this connection ever since we met as if our hearts were always meant to be one, which they were since the Absolute made us for each other.

Anyways, we go down and celebrate with our people and then rest for the night before we begin to head out. My mother flies at me to hug me as we are making our way to them.

"You can't leave without giving your mother and father goodbye hugs and kisses," she says.

"We were coming to you to do just that, mother. Why do you always have to act like we don't?" I ask.

"Because I love embarrassing you in front of your wife."

"Come on, honey. Let them go," my father says.

"Fine."

"I'm sure I don't need to say this but be careful with Absalom and the vainglory that gives him his powers."

"You already know that he is being aided by the vainglory?" I ask.

"What else could boost his conceited powers besides demonic powers? His allies also seemed possessed and not themselves when his specters merged with their bodies. Absalom spoke of peace, but his allies were quick to violence after an exchange of few words."

"Figures. We'll do our best, mother and father."

"We already know you will, but you should reassure our citizens that you will obtain victory for them and bring justice to Absalom."

"We don't have time for speeches. Absalom could be mobilizing his forces right now."

"Well, it's a good thing that we have soldiers guarding the walls and scouting the streets while people are gathering in the main hall ready to hear your speech."

"What? How did you-nevermind. I guess I have no choice now."

"That's right," my mother says.

I almost forgot that mother can echo her voice throughout the city and father can give commands to people through his thoughts. What am I even going to say?

Going to the main hall, I see what must be hundreds of people trying to squeeze in with lots more people outside. Looking behind me, I see Kyla and my parents smiling at me. They must be silently cheering and praying for me in their minds. I feel an empowering force emanate from them, so I nod and smile back before facing the crowd. Well, here goes nothing.

"Faithful citizens of Simbiosi, justice for the conceited Absalom is at hand. Soon, you will no longer have to worry about him, his influence, and the vainglory that manifests through his powers. Princess Kyla and I will have his head or him on his knees begging for mercy from the Absolute. Remember that even when this is over, the constant battle of life doesn't end and we still have more enemies to bring to justice, so stay vigilant, stay strong, and keep fighting for truth and love!"

Everyone cheers and claps for me despite my simple speech. I was never good at giving speeches, which is why I let Kyla do all the talking during political discussions and times when we need to say speeches. Regardless, I'm glad that what I said was appreciated by everyone. Kyla and I say our goodbyes to my parents before leaving to finally face Absalom in person. Justice will finally be coming to him, the idiotic pitiable sinner. He'll get what's coming to him for what he's done to everyone I love.

*Concept art for Absalom and his specters

Chapter 4 – The Absolute's Love

Caleb used to be sleepy as we traveled our way here. Now, he's awake and focused. Absalom's city is in the distance. It sits upon an inactive volcano and is surrounded by what must be hundreds of thousands of specters that fly around it like a tornado. The sky is covered in black clouds that swirl around as if something bad is going to happen. Sure enough, Absalom approaches us by using one of his specters to speak to us.

"You're going to wish that you took my offer and died in the battle against my allies and specters because I won't kill you in this battle. Instead, I'll sacrifice you to add to my power just like I'm doing with the men, women, and rebellious children around me right now," Absalom says.

"Don't do it!" I say.

"It's too late. You can probably hear their screaming from where you are."

It's true. I can hear and feel their screams in my soul even though they must be far away from us. The tornado of specters grows fiercer and black lightning starts flashing in the sky.

"You've crossed the line and you'll pay for what you've done!" Caleb says.

"I thank you for the inspiration. Your power has shown me that I need more to beat you. I also have to concede that you're right in that violence is needed in some cases to bring about true peace. These people were threats to that peace whether you think so or not. No price is too high for peace and the people you love after all. I'm sure you agree. Now, enough talk. Behold my power and despair."

"I don't think we will. Caleb!"

"You're the one who's going to despair at our power!" Caleb says before taking my hand.

Together we say, "Beg for mercy from the Absolute, all you conceited sinners! Judgment has arrived!"

Our dragon combines itself in a flash of golden light before it breathes its golden and black fire at the incoming specters and the conceited. It then spirals around the inactive volcano to create a tornado of flames. While it does this, we defend it from its attackers on top of its body until the entire volcano is covered in gold and black flames and many of the conceited and specters are burned to ash. The clouds have also somewhat cleared so that the sun can shine down in places. Seeing that it's safe to go down, we head straight to the castle that sits on the volcano, where Absalom must be.

Going into the castle, we find it mysteriously quiet. Be careful, Kyla. I know, Caleb. There are probably more enemies around here somewhere. Also, I know it's okay to admit you're starting to feel tired. Though that battle was short, the power to make that tornado took a lot out of you and me. It sure did. Hey, when this is over, do you want to finally start to have children? Why bring it up now? I'm not doing it, Kyla. Neither am I, Caleb. I guess it's on both of our minds. I guess so, Kyla. So, do you? I think it's a good idea, especially since there aren't any threats like Absalom around that need our immediate attention and it would be good to let our armies do the work for once rather than just being peacekeepers.

Let's try then when we get back home and after the celebration. I'd love to have two daughters and two sons.

You know what I'd like, Kyla. Four sons and three daughters. Or we could have four daughters and four sons, Caleb. Who am I kidding? The Absolute decides this, so let's hope and pray for the best. Thank you for bringing it up. We both did. With something that we really want now in our minds, we both feel invigorated with more energy to wipe away our tiredness for the time being.

There's still no sign of anyone in this castle. The sound of nothing but our footsteps and the footsteps of our dragon is deafening. To our surprise, we don't face any resistance even when we enter the throne room and find Absalom waiting for us without any of his specters around him.

"What? Decided to give up?" Caleb asks.

"No, not at all. I've just been busy using my specters to keep more of my citizens inside so they don't fight you. Believe it or not, I didn't intend for any of them to attack you. I only wanted my specters to do that,"

Absalom says. "Now, with the innocent out of the way, we can have a proper fight."

To start the fight, our dragon breathes its blue and red flames on Absalom who uses a seemingly endless supply of specters to shield him. We attack him on both sides and even now, he conjures more specters to defend him and fight against us. Seeing that our tactic isn't working, our dragon ceases its flames and we back away to quickly think of a new plan. What can we possibly do, Caleb? Use the dragon's gold and black flames, I guess, Kyla? It's risky and may completely deplete us of our strength especially since he's concentrated all his power into himself. Better than tiring ourselves on his defenses. Maybe.

"Are you done? You've yet to bring me to my knees despite all my specters that you managed to dispel. Remember that damage done to them is damage done to me and see that I still stand unshaken and uninjured," Absalom says before turning his head and eyes to the side. "No. I thought…I thought I had all of…"

Two people enter the room from behind us and stand defending Absalom. They are cloaked in darkness and specters that defend them from their sides and back. The darkness cloaking them dispels a bit to reveal that one is a woman and the other a boy that's about ten years younger than us.

"What are you two doing here? I thought I said to stay safe in your rooms," Absalom says to them.

"I couldn't let you fight this threat by yourself," the woman says who must be his wife.

"We can help you, father," the boy says.

"We love you and make sure your dream comes true."

"You're my hero, father. Let's put these villains down."

"Okay, okay. Just make my specters do most of the fighting," Absalom says as he begrudgingly accepts their help.

"Yes, my love."

"As you command, my father."

Somethings wrong. I have a feeling the conceited are possessing them in a strange way, Kyla. Me too, Caleb. Try not to hurt them too much. Of course not. We let our dragon coat the room in red and blue flames to keep away Absalom's wife and son as it tries to purify them. Meanwhile, we fight against Absalom's specters who are more fully formed now. These specters look like skeletal knights with horns on their heads. They wield various kinds of heavy swords, axes, and halberds in an effort to overwhelm us with their strength and end the fight quickly.

The fight seemingly goes nowhere with Absalom's side slowly whittling down our strength. That is until Absalom's wife manages to get in front of Kyla and starts to fight her while Absalom's son fights Caleb. Absalom is sure to overwhelm us like this. Let's risk holding these two down while our dragon purifies them, Kyla. I'm afraid that's the only thing we can do too, Caleb. It may intensify Absalom's aggression, but if these two wake up from their possession, they could get Absalom to stand down. That's what I'm thinking.

We take this risk and hold down these two in front of our dragon as it breathes its fire on us. Absalom tries sending as many of his specters against us, and even though our dragon's flames don't hurt us and act as a shield, some of his specters' attacks get through and we have to suffer being cut and stabbed by their attacks. Eventually, the presence of the conceited is gone from Absalom's wife and son, except…something is wrong. Deeply wrong. Can you feel it too, Caleb? I can, Kyla. They're dead but they haven't turned to ash. It's like…they been dead this whole time, and not only that. Their souls are in…

"Get away from them!" Absalom says as he pushes us to the back of the room with a flood of specters.

To defend ourselves from this flood, our dragon has to use its gold and black flames and use the rest of our energy to mitigate the damage. By the end of it, our dragon is separated into two and our strength has reached its limits. Meanwhile, Absalom whispers to his wife and son as he tries in vain to wake them up. Caleb and I look at each other before slowly approaching him.

"Absalom, they're dead and have been for a while. What have you done to them?" I ask.

"I haven't done anything and they have been alive! They were at least…until you killed them!" he says.

"They've been dead, you dolt! Wake up from your self-delusions if you have any sense left in you," Caleb says.

"I gave them the constant protection of my specters. I would've known if they were dead!"

"You don't have full control of them because they don't always follow your orders," I say. "The attacks on our home, your allies not listening to you, and you not even being able to hold back these two from coming here. Face it. The vainglory are manifesting themselves through your specters and are using you for their own ends. They aren't communicating to you everything. Least of all the deaths of your wife and son who are now…now, in the Land of the Forgotten."

"That's not true! It can't-"

Before he can finish, I touch his wife and use my other hand to touch Absalom so that he knows what I do. I'm able to sense the destination of a heart if I touch their body and his wife's soul is damned along with the soul of his son who was at the age of reason.

"You made them conceited, Absalom. Their souls were in a state of falsehood, of grievous mortal sin and they accepted it because of you. You helped damn their souls and the vainglory kept their minds in a state of sin," I say.

"I…I…" Absalom says unable to make an excuse.

I can feel his shriveled heart slowly begin to beat more as he begins to cry and regret what he's done. Turning around to Caleb, I see that he's dropped his guard. Absalom is obviously defeated and doesn't seem to want to fight anymore.

"Do it then. Punish me for my failure," Absalom says.

Caleb and I step back from him while our dragons burn him with their flames. By the end of it, his crown is gone along with the black cloak and the hole in his chest is no longer there. He's somehow deserving of the Absolute's mercy much to Caleb's and my surprise. Suddenly, Absalom's body convulses. He curls up on the spot as specters come out of him and then disappear.

"Get out of here! The vainglory are furious at my repentance and are trying to manifest themselves," Absalom says.

With our dragons, we try to defuse the situation with more fire, but this ceases Absalom's convulsing for a few seconds before it begins again. We then try using our weapons, however, this doesn't work either as specters manifest to defend him and push us back.

"Save yourselves and leave me to my penance!" Absalom says before using his specters to push us out of his castle along with our dragons.

"Come on, Kyla! We must go!" Caleb says.

Seeing as there's nothing we can do, we ride our dragons far away from the inactive volcano until an explosion rocks the entire land, and black and white made of specters shield the city that lies on top of it. This shield is unbreakable as neither our dragons nor are attacks can make a dent in it.

"We should have soldiers guarding this thing," Caleb suggests.

"I agree. Do you think Absalom is still alive inside of it?" I ask.

"Probably. I don't know really. All I know is that he made an act of perfect repentance, so even if he's dead, his soul will be purified and then sent to the Land of the True."

"Yeah, and despite everything that he's done, I hope that's the case."

"Yeah…"

Now that our job is done, we head back home much to the joy of our people. We tell them of what happened and a force of soldiers is sent out to guard the shield of specters. Also, we tell them that we're taking a break to start a family, and the leaders of the kingdom agree and think that it's an appropriate reward for us after all that we've done. A celebration is then held for us at which we are required to give a speech much to Caleb's dismay.

War, Love, and the Absolute

I start the speech by saying, "Though we are glad for our victory, we mourn the lost at the same time. Absalom was a man afflicted by tragedy and buckled under the weight of it despite being one of the greatest self-sacrificing soldiers of his kingdom. During the last time we saw him, I revealed to him that his wife and son were in the Land of the Forgotten as a result of his actions and he repented of his sins and did his penance. Even now, his shield holds him in a makeshift prison where I believe he is doing his penance. This should remind us that the Absolute always gives us a chance to repent despite our many flaws and what we do and that even the worst of us are not beyond redemption. Days and years may seem the same and our situation may get worse but remember that love and truth remain constant and so will our promise to the Absolute and to you that we will do the best for you as your prince and princess of Simbiosi."

The people clap and await Caleb's addition to my speech. All eyes including mine are on him forcing him to get up and not hide in his chair.

"What else do I need to add to that wonderful speech?" Caleb adds much to everyone's amusement. "My wife and I went out and did our job and despite everything that's happened, we didn't learn anything new and weren't challenged in any meaningful way, in my opinion. We were just the Absolute's tools in Absalom's conversion. There's nothing of note of me to reflect on either than one thing. Life is a constant battle. We stumble, fall, and get back up repeatedly. Though we know there's an end to it, we never know how long we must hold out and sometimes may lose ourselves in the process like Absalom did. I only ask that you don't lose yourselves. Remember who the Absolute made you to be. We are all made to be saints. Remember the endless mercy that the Absolute contains and is willing to give to all. We are unworthy of it, but the Absolute is waiting to give it to us like a father waiting on the porch for a wayward child. Through this war that we call life, we will sanctify ourselves and the world. Empowered by love and truth, we will make it to the Land of the True together."

This speech gets the crowd to stand, cheer, and clap even more than my speech much to Caleb's surprise. The rest of the celebration goes well and Caleb even willingly dances with me and seems to have fun doing it. It's a good start for the restful times that we will raise a family in. As the slow music starts to play, I kiss Caleb and rest my head on his chest while slowly dancing with him thankful for everything I have, everyone around me, and everything that I've been through that's made me stronger.

The End

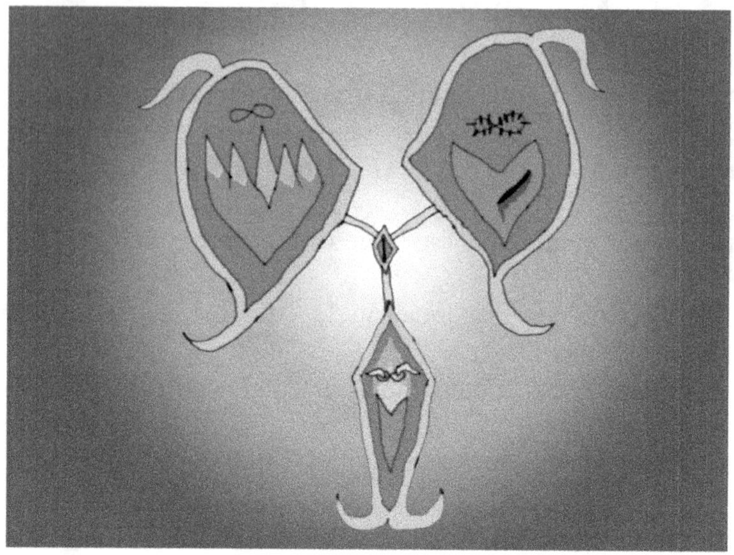

*Concept art for a representation of the Absolute. The left half represents truth's dominion over all, the right side represents suffering for someone being the greatest show of love, and the bottom part represents the enlightenment of the Absolute and how it ignites the heart with true love.

War, Love, and the Absolute

- The dragon of mercy's appearance is inspired by the Blue Eyes White Dragon, the dragon of justice's appearance is inspired by the Red Eyes Black Dragon, and the Judgment of the Absolute dragon's appearance is inspired by the Judgment Dragon. All these dragon inspirations are from *Yu-Gi-Oh!* by Konami and Kazuki Takahashi.

- This was the first story that came to my mind in this series. I was going to make it the only one, but then more stories came to me.

- Absalom's castle that's sat on an inactive volcano is inspired by the Volcano Manor from *Elden Ring* by From Software.

- What I wanted to do with this series was to have the main character of the next story be in the one before it. As you have seen, Caleb and Kyla were in the previous story, so Absalom will be in the next.

A Lack of Heart: A Kingdom for One
Albert Oon

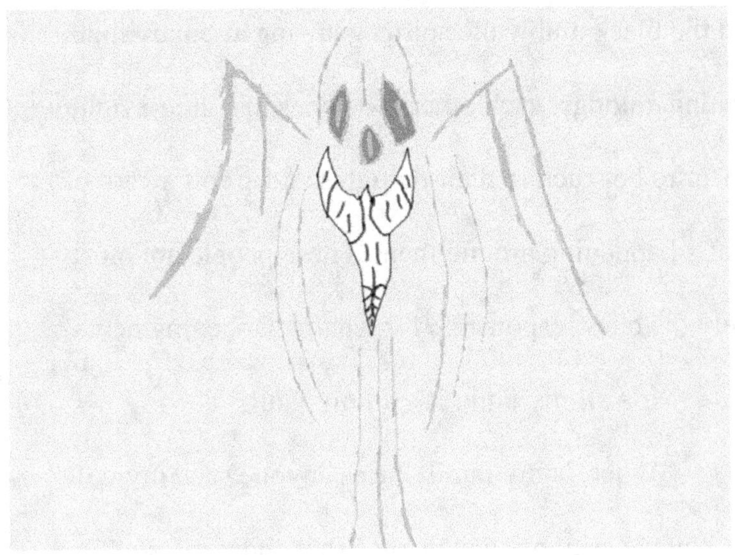

Chapter 1 – Broken and Scattered

Where am I? Who am I? I've just fallen from the

sky after being launched from the top of the inactive

volcano that has a ruined city on it. How do I know what it

is? What about this barrier of hundreds of thousands of

white and black spirits that reaches up to the sky?

Where am I? Who am I? In my chest, I feel a pull to

answer these questions first so I can know what I should be

doing, but first, where should I go? The tug in my heart

tells me to go in a direction and I go to it. In this direction, I find the black and white spirits gnawing at bones and fighting amongst each other. The ones that aren't fighting appear to be stuck in their thoughts and aren't aware of what's happening around them. These people are most likely the ones responsible for what's happening here.

"It's all my fault, it's all my fault."

"Where's my family? Has anyone seen my wife? Has anyone seen my daughter? What about my son?"

"Rally with me and we'll make the world a better peaceful place without wars! If you won't be with me, you are against me and will pay the price for doing so!"

"Kill me. Can someone kill me or put me in prison? I deserve worse than Hell. I deserve worse than being forgotten forever."

What is this insanity that's going around? These spirits are so fractured and keep repeating the same things over and over. I guess everyone here is like that including me. Coming across a broken mirror, I find that I'm fractured as well. My scarred chest in the shape of a heart is the only body part that I have. Besides it, I have three big light grey eyes, what seems to be a crown on my head, grey wings, grey claws, and a grey flowing robe. All of it is grey. Why is every part of me like this? Who or what am I?

The answer to my questions is close. My heart is magnetized to it as it's a servant to a kind master. I now stand in front of a small house with many weapons and shields in front of it. This must be the home of a blacksmith by the looks of it. Going into it, a find a small child playing with makeshift figures of knights, princesses, and horned spirits.

"I'll be the protector! When they need help, they need only call and I'll be there to lend a hand or my sword!"

What a fascinating boy. His face seems to glow like the sun. When I reach my arm out to him, his essence enters me and everything around me changes. I am in the place of the boy and the world around me is no longer grey.

"Absalom," I hear a woman call out.

Absalom. Is that me? My body moves and gets up at the woman's call and goes outside to the woman who called me.

"Yes, mother?" I say to her excitedly without intentionally meaning to speak.

So, my name is Absalom and this is my mother. She's a woman that seems like the sun is always shining on her. Her clothes are made of some kind of beast and look like they have chainmail in them. A colorful crown that's made of paper and grass sits on her head. Looking at it makes me proud, which means I must've made it for her.

"Father is going to be home soon from hunting. Get the table ready for him," my mother says.

"There's no need," I hear a man's voice.

War, Love, and the Absolute

Turning around, I see the man who is presumably my father. He's a large muscular man covered in heavy armor and blood. On one of his shoulders sits a deer and on his other shoulder sits a wolf. He carries an unsheathed knife and sword on his hips and on his back is a chipped shield. A crown of chainmail sits on his head and he seems to shine like the sun because of his armor.

"Are you okay?!" my mother asks.

"I am. Are you worried about the blood? Don't worry, this is mostly their blood. I've only been scratched thanks to my armor," my father says before laughing.

"Of course he's okay. My father is the master blacksmith of the world!" I say.

"That's right! Speaking of my works, where is your brother?"

"Still trying to replicate your work."

"I've told that boy that he needs to stop trying to replicate what I do and make his own. The Absolute has gifted us all with unique gifts and I expect him to make better work than I can."

"And I'll be a great protector of you, mother, and brother!"

"Of course you will! You'll become a great hero that many will sing stories of! I can see it already as if the Absolute has granted me a vision of the future."

I'll make you proud. Huh? What's that noise? I hear silent cries and screaming. Who could be making that noise? It doesn't matter to me right now. I want to see my older brother, listen to his stories, and watch him work. Before I know it, we're out hunting together.

"If father can kill a deer and the wolf hunting it, we can do the same or even better," my brother says.

"Yes, we can!" I say.

We stalk through the forests looking for prey and watching out for predators. My older brother looks like he blends into the forest with the many leaves on his armor and his green and brown face paint. Eventually, we hear the

sounds of something in the forest, get excited, and go to it

to find a pack of wolves eating the remains of a rival pack

of wolves. They turn their attention to us before my brother

grabs me and tells me to run.

"I'll hold them off for you!" he says while pushing

me ahead of him.

Since he knows best, I run away, but I have second

thoughts when I see that he's surrounded. I go back running

to him while reaching out to him. This is when specters in

the form of legless knights appear and fight off the wolves

with swords, spears, and shields.

"You have…you have your Heart Absolute ability!

That's amazing, Absalom," my brother says.

There's a slight hint of jealousy in his voice that I

ignore since I'm confident that my brother should be

getting his Heart Absolute ability soon enough if he doesn't

have it already. Hearing about this ability reminds me of it.

People obtain it at certain times some earlier than others. The ability is also different ranging from being good at basic jobs to more amazing abilities like mine. Every factor of it is based on our heart made by the Absolute and when we aren't ourselves, we become conceited and our abilities become an inversion of our real one or a pale imitation of what we want our talents to be.

Now that I have my Heart Absolute ability, I daydream of what I could do with them. Immediately, these daydreams transition to me helping people and then to a small group of royal soldiers arriving at my home. With them are clergy that are dressed in such a way that makes me doubt their vows of poverty with their ornamental outfits designed with hearts on it similar to the armor of the royal soldiers. They've heard of my abilities and want me to go with them so I can hone my heart's ability and protect even more people. I immediately accept the offer without question. Turning around I say goodbye to my family who are proud of me, but before heading out, I hear the same screaming and crying from before, but it's a bit louder this time.

The change of scenery reveals the source of this screaming and crying as I am now fighting on a battlefield or rather, I'm hardly fighting while my specters do the work for me. When they take damage, I feel their pain, however, even though they are stabbed through the chest and head, burned, and blown up, I don't suffer any major injuries. In battle, I can summon seven specters, but this never feels like it's enough, so I push myself to summon three more. Doing this takes its toll on the other specters who aren't as strong as they were. Still, I am told that I am one of the Absolute's most valued soldiers and am crowned and celebrated as such.

Huh? What's going on? I can see hear the screaming and crying, and it's louder this time. At this celebration, everyone but one woman stops in place as if time has affected everyone but us. We look into each other's eyes and soon after, I'm transported to us getting married, having children, and then…I'm alone in a burning forest. Where's my family? Huh…there are heads of my family in the dirt and body parts buried as well. My son…my wife…my father, mother, and brother…The screaming and crying are even louder than it was before.

Wait! Hold on! Stop! I'm in battle again, but this time I feel a sense of unquenchable rage. These people are responsible for the deaths of my family and friends. No matter how many I bring to justice and how many honors I get at the celebration after, I feel a chasm in my heart that can't be filled that is until I see another woman, however, I come back to the same scene with my family buried in the ground, this time with her and my daughter being among the bodies, and again the screaming and crying gets louder until I finally realize the tears coming down my face and that the screaming and crying is coming from me.

"Please…stop…not again," I say.

"This is not even your worst failure," a disembodied voice says.

"Don't remind me of it!"

I feel like I know what the voice is talking about and am struggling to keep it out of my head and forget what I just remembered.

"Twice you lost your family. Twice there wasn't enough for you to bury. Twice your friends, leaders, and the Church promised you they would be protected from the conceited, and twice they failed. Twice you prayed to the Absolute for their protection and many times over your prayers fell on deaf ears."

"Shut up! I'll kill you if you say another word."

Manifesting out of thin air, a man with green and grey eyes appears in front of me. This man has half a face, and half a body, and floats in the air like the specters I've seen. Something about him reminds me of myself even though none of his features are like the faces of myself that I've seen in reflections so far. There's something unnatural about him.

"I wish I could kill myself as well. Regardless, I will tell you what you need to hear. You went mad after the death of your second wife and first daughter, especially since you decided to marry again and have another child, a baby boy. In your mind, there was no cost too high to pay for their protection. Darkened by the temptations of the vainglory, you sacrificed your arms and people who you decided were guilty so that you could spawn an army of specters to protect the world with. You recruited many people. Many people also were damned to the Land of the Forgotten as a result including your new family."

Hearing this gives me flashes of when it happened. When a servant of the Absolute made me feel the cold and forgotten fates of my family and when I was brought to justice.

"What is this then? Am I dead? Is this the Land of Purification before I am sent to the Land of the True or am I in the Land of the Forgotten?"

"Neither though you deserve to be forgotten forever for your crimes and failures. You're a failure of a brother, son, friend, father, and husband, especially for leading two of your family members and your supporters to eternal damnation. Who can live with a sin like that on their soul?"

He's right. How can I live with this much failure? Remembering it all puts a weight on my heart that feels like it can crush it any second now.

"Just because you fail, it doesn't mean that you can't get up again," the voice of my mother says as I remember it.

"Failure is not the end. The Absolute gives us as many second chances as we need," my father's voice rings in my ears.

"I fail all the time," my brother says, "We'll never be perfect in this life, but we can always get better."

I remember that. It's hard to believe, yet I still remember it and believe it to some extent.

"I may have failed, but I'm still alive, which means it's not over yet," I say.

"So what? Can you live with your failures for the rest of your life? Can you do enough penance to pay for what you've done?"

"To be honest, I don't feel like I can, but the Absolute has judged that I stay alive to try. I may have failed my family with my recent actions. Not again. I will never fail them again from this moment on."

As I speak, the other me is absorbed into my body until I am one with my other self. The scenery around me has changed back to the blacksmith's house. I'm back in the city that sits on the inactive volcano, the place I wanted to start my empire peace at. Turning around, I look into my reflection in a shield and see my half face and half of my torso with half a heart shape cut out of it. It's an ugly sight to behold not just because most of me is missing, but because it's my face, the face of a vile sinner. Nevertheless, I embrace it and will have to live with it. There's much work to do to put myself back together and right my wrongs.

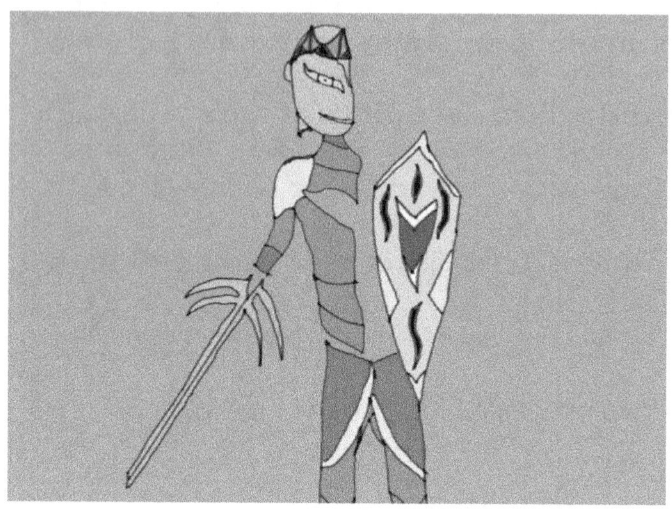

Chapter 2 - Break off all Vexations

The feeling that guided me to part of myself is quieter now if quieter is a good word for the feeling. It's vaguer and completely silent at points. Many of the specters around me now notice me and senselessly attack me forcing me to defend myself from manifestations of myself. With each specter I defeat, the more of myself I remember, and the way forward is made clearer. It's a mixed blessing if I'm being honest.

Every memory brings back the pains of the past that affect my specters that I use to defend myself. My specters lose their knight appearance and look more like disfigured bodies some of which bear a resemblance to my dead family. They remind me of my failures and even speak with a distorted version of their voices mixed with mine.

"I love you," I hear my first and second wives say.

"The hero you could've become…what happened?" my mother asks.

"Where's the good son that I raised?" my father asks.

"Daddy!" my children say.

Something's wrong with these specters. They defend me and then talk without me commanding them to. Am I doing this on my own or is it something else? Currently, I'm going up the volcano since that's where I came down from. I'm beginning to notice that some of the specters here are different than the others. Some wear black and gold crowns and have tinges of grey on their body. It seems like these specters reflect the worst parts of me so I try to ignore them, however, a group of them gathers around a gate near the top of the volcano.

"There's no point in penance," one of the specters says.

"I am perfect as I am."

"There's nothing more to change."

"I'll just fail again. I might as well just do what I'm best at and bear my flaws."

This doesn't seem right. I know that a person who is true to themselves will try to perfect themselves and be the person that the Absolute originally made them to be. A person true to themselves shouldn't accept mediocrity, and I shouldn't either. My family wanted me to be more. As if reading my thoughts, the specters stop talking and look at me with angry looks on their faces before swarming from all directions to attack me.

My specters form a protective barrier around me, but I can't keep this up, especially with the constant noise in my head tempting me to give up. What can I do? Who can I call for help? Perhaps the Absolute is the only one who can, so I say a silent prayer. For a few seconds, I think my prayer falls on deaf ears until I see that the specters fall one by one until they're all gone. When I dissipate my barrier of specters, I see that my savior is an angelic being made of various kinds of shields, swords, knives, and arrows all of which appear worn down from battle. Is this my guardian angel, a servile of the Absolute? A feeling within me makes me think that I know this servile somehow.

"It's been a while since you last asked for my help and help from the Absolute. I'm glad that you did," the servile says.

My feelings of gratitude soon give way to feelings of bitterness after remembering all the times that I thought the Absolute would've helped me and that being devoted to the Absolute means being His tool. A lot of representations of serviles show them as being humanlike whereas others show them as an amalgamation of tools, weapons, plants, or whatever else they may be helping with.

"Yeah...thank you," I struggle to say.

"I'll protect you from the vainglory and help you regain yourself. We should be quick since the vainglory will not stop until you're theirs again."

I remember being under their control and their almost divine appearance. They manifest themselves as grey and gold beings, with wings, and horn-like crowns. Their tempting whispers became one in my mind when I sacrificed the people that I considered to be my enemies for power and they still whisper to me right now. Suddenly, my guardian servile puts its sword through my head and takes out several of the vainglories from my body before dissipating them.

"Thank...thank you," I say.

"You're welcome. As I said, we should move. More from the surrounding area are already on the attack as you can see," my guardian servile says before moving up the volcano.

Following its advice, I follow the servile all the way up the volcano and into the castle that sits at its peak. Memories of what happened here force their way into my head and remind me that the third family I had was damned to the Land of the Forgotten because of me. The feelings of guilt and regret are enough to stop me in my place until my guardian servile repels more vainglories from me.

"Hurry inside!" it says.

After doing as it says, I can feel myself being drawn to the throne room. My body moves by itself as I go there and find an armored version of myself that only has half a face, half a body, one leg, and a sword for an arm.

"Here, again? Do you think that liar with you will change anything?" the specter of myself says.

"I'm not here to argue with you," I say while summoning ten specters.

"You must be because surely you can't be here to fight me." The specter of myself summons enough specters to fill the entire room. "This is the power I have, or rather, you had when I was complete and conceited. You are nothing more than a specter for me to consume so I can resume my war for peace in this world of endless wars and conflicts. The entire world will be my kingdom where the innocent can live without fear for their lives. Hurry up and be one with me again."

The specter me sends a seemingly endless number of specters at me and soon enough, I'm consumed in the flood. Everything is dark and I can hardly hear anything except the faint voice of my guardian servile.

"Why resist? Why not become a king?"

"I'm not worthy of becoming one nor am I fit to be one."

"I am the worthiest person in the world. No one has the same abilities, experience, and the ability to deal with as much heartache as I do."

"There is no one who is as foolish as I."

"I don't need the Absolute. I even had the vainglory under my control."

"I had the illusion of control."

"To be free from the Absolute is the freedom to define myself, and I am Absalom, the one true King of All! Under my protection, no more innocent people will suffer. I will finally live in peace with a loving family. All I need to do is free this world from the Absolute's grasp and I can have it all. I was on the verge of making it happen."

"All I do falls to ruin."

"What would I rather think? Don't I deserve the glory that comes with my power or am I the sum of my failures?"

Considering the options, I decide, "I will not be a slave to my high opinions of myself, especially when I've been proven wrong. How can I be so prideful when I've fallen so far from what I was even in comparison to what I want myself to be at the height of my power? It was right for me to fail and be given this punishment. Let the Absolute do whatever it wants with me."

The space around me clears as my specters enter me and the vainglories fly away before disappearing into thin air.

"Well done. Your humility has banished a majority of the demonic presence of your heart," my guardian servile says.

"How come you didn't help me more?" I ask.

"I brought your prayers to the Absolute and prayed for you. I've always been at your side and aiding you even though it may not be obvious."

War, Love, and the Absolute

It isn't obvious at all. Still, I'm glad that it seems to be over, or at least mostly over. The barrier surrounding the volcano has many holes in it allowing the light outside to shine through and a lot of the specters from the city are coming back into me. I look at myself in the reflective surface of the floor to see the tan color in my skin has been restored along with the color in my eyes. My hair is back and my body is mostly restored except for a heart-shaped hole in my chest and the other half of my face. Where could the last part of me be?

"Follow me to find the last piece," my guardian servile says as if it read my mind.

Since I have no better option and feel that I can trust the servile more, I do so. Hopefully, with its help, I'll finally be free of this prison and be more of the person my family envisioned me to be.

Chapter 3 - A Pathetic Sin

"We're almost there," a specter of mine in the streets says.

"Hurry."

"Complete the penance."

"Do mother, father, and brother proud."

"Be the father and husband you were meant to be."

Ever since my act of humility, every specter in the streets has been encouraging me, being positive, and willingly joining me. There are no vainglories in sight, yet there has to be one or something close by to get rid of so I can be done with this cleansing. My guardian servile guides me from the top of the volcano to the bottom where the sewers are, which is a fitting place for a sinful being to be now that I think about it. It's a smelly and dark place that only gets darker the further we travel and the only light is my guardian who emanates a strange dim light that is somehow brighter than the darkness.

Curious about this, I ask, "What is that light shining from you?"

"It's not a light shining from me. It's the light of the Absolute or rather the darkness of the Absolute that is brighter than the light of evil," my guardian servile explains.

"That's interesting for you to say since there's no light here."

"What you see is the light of evil that's coming from the last part of you that is weak to it. It's just that the light of evil is exposed as the darkness it is when the darkness of the Absolute is close to it."

"What is this darkness of the Absolute?"

"It's a darkness that tests the faithful and the same darkness that's been trapping you here. Many times you have failed, but now you are on the edge of victory. Don't let the people you love and who love you down. I'm here for you."

My guardian servile disappears along with the light it had. The darkness around me engulfs me and the silence deafens me until I hear the sound of someone, probably the last specter of myself, crying. Sure enough, after following the sound of the crying, I see a dim light coming from a specter of myself huddled in a corner.

"What's the use? I'll just fail again. I might lose another family. I'll probably be too late to protect the innocent."

"But-"

"Everyone is tested by the Absolute until death. I can't establish peace by myself or with the help of others. Even if I do help make the world for the better, a generation or two in the future can ruin it."

"Don't think like that."

"I'm not wrong. There's no use in trying. I won't be perfect in this life. I may fail my next family or disappoint someone that trusted me."

"No one is perfect."

"But I'm expected to be. The Absolute wants the best of us even if mercy is always available until death, and above all, I fail the Absolute first with every sin. What's even the use when my prayers and acts of devotion fall flat when the Absolute wishes to test me by allowing me to fall into sin?"

There's no use arguing with him when he keeps despairing about what could happen. What am I going to do to change myself? Perhaps that's the problem. I can't change myself. I have corrupted myself, but my true self still exists. The only one who knows who that is made my heart and loves me like no other, the Absolute. With my one and only option clear, I place my heart and soul into the hands of the Absolute promising that I'll be who I'm meant to be for both the Lord of my heart and the people placed under my care.

Once this promise is made, light emanates from my chest and the heart-shaped hole is restored along with the rest of my body. I exit the sewers to see that the barrier is gone. What somewhat surprises me is that I see an army encamped around the volcano. It makes sense since I was a dangerous individual. I'll talk to them soon enough, but first, I go to a nearby river to look at my restored appearance. Part of me still feels disgusted by the man I see, especially since I lack arms, however, I see glimpses of a better man in the reflection. I'll make sure that this better man is me by the end of my life.

Well, I guess it's time to see what this army will do to me. Portals in the sky open up and two dragons come through them. One dragon is light blue while the other is crimson red. The riders of these dragons are the ones that brought me both mercy and justice, and true servants of the Absolute. Along with them is a young man with black hair and gold and red garments. He must be the one who made the portals for them. They land in front of me with small groups from the army not too far behind them.

"Prince Caleb, Princess Kyla," I say as I bow my head.

"Absalom. It looks like you found yourself," Caleb says.

"Yes, I have and emerged reborn through the Absolute's trials. Now, I guess it's time for me to face another trial from the world."

Caleb and Kyla look at each other before Kyla says, "You won't face any trial or any punishment from us, any of our allies, or the Church."

"The barrier you were in was a penitential punishment from the Absolute for a little over a year, and if He let you go free, then who are we to reimprison you?" Caleb continues, "Come. We'll give you back your crown, arms, and a new place in the world."

"Really?" I ask in surprise.

"Of course. The people of Simbiosi are charitable, especially to the repentant. Think of this as paying your debt to us."

"Yes. I will honorably serve you. My specters and this kingdom of mine is yours."

"Save it for the ceremony."

I take Caleb's advice and save my thanks for the Absolute for my crowning ceremony. The entire thing is more or less a show of the Absolute's mercy to the citizens of Simbiosi to remind them what it is and I'm the fool on stage confessing my heart out that they respectfully clap for as if it were a play. Caleb and Kyla also talk as well and are credited by the Church for the part they played in repentance. Nevertheless, I'm humbled by the public confession, crowning, and acceptance of my service. In addition to the crown I once had, I am given a pair of metal arms that work as if they were my normal arms, however, Caleb says that they'll stop working if I become conceited again, which I hope never happens again.

After the ceremony, I'm allowed to talk to people after it and a sense of this happening before hits me. I don't know why that is. Perhaps it's because I met my first and second wives at parties. No woman here catches my eye like they did so it's most likely my imagination. Once everything here is done, I am escorted by Caleb and Kyla to their castle where I'll be staying. Along the way, we hear a woman crying for help. We go to help and find some criminals trying to rob her house. I immediately jump into action and overwhelm the criminals with ten of my specters before going to check on the woman.

There's something about her that captivates my eyes and she seems captivated by me as well. It's as if I can see the beauty of her soul. This feeling is similar to the feeling I had when I saw my other wives but different somehow.

"Hello. Um. Thank you for saving me," she says.

"The honor is mine. What's your name?" I ask.

"Estrella."

"My name is Absalom."

"I've heard of you. Is-"

"No, no," Caleb interrupts, "You can't just come back from your penance and find another wife, especially after you lost three."

"It's okay, Caleb. Let them be. We have to bring these criminals to jail," Kyla says.

"…okay. Fine, but don't you rush it, Absalom!"

Caleb and Kyla summon their dragons to aid them in taking the criminals to jail while leaving Estrella and me alone together.

"Let me help you clean up what the criminals broke," I say.

"Thank you, but as Prince Caleb said, every wife you've had has died," Estrella says.

"Yes, it's true. I'm not asking for your hand in marriage right now. I just want to help."

"You said 'right now'. Does that mean you'll ask later? We've just met."

"I-uh. Would you give me the honor of spending a few days together first before I ask?"

"Again, you're making it sound like you're already planning on marrying me."

She's got me there as if she can see the desire for a family deep within my heart. Despite knowing this, she seems amused and is brightly smiling at me.

"Okay, I confess that one of the desires of my heart is to have a family or at the very least a group of friends I can consider family."

"We can enjoy the day together once the house is…clean?"

"While we were talking, I had my specters clean up the house. Now, it looks like nothing happened to it at all. In fact, it looks like it recently had a cleaning done."

"You must be really anxious to have people to be close to."

"Yet again, you got me there. Can you read hearts?"

"No. Unfortunately, my Heart Absolute ability is to strengthen people with my singing voice."

"I'd love to hear you sing."

"Maybe if we find a place that lets us and if you sing with me."

"It's a deal. Shall we go?"

"Yes."

With that, Estrella and I are off to spend as much of the day together as possible. Though the dark shadow of my past is behind me, it's just that. Behind me, and always will be from now on. I won't let my past define my future or how I act now other than remembering my mistakes to learn from them. Truth and love will now be my goal in life that I will be devoted to no matter how many times I may fail in the future.

Albert Oon

The End

War, Love, and the Absolute

Behind the Story

- This story is inspired by *Dead Cells* by Motion Twin.

- Chapter 2's title, Break off all Vexations, is a reference to the lyrics of the song, *Mirror of the World*, by Daisuke Ishiwatari from the game *Guilty Gear Strive* by Arc System Works. The song itself inspired the themes of the story a bit and fit the story, especially the lyrics in the song talking about God. Speaking of the lyrics, I was going to have a part where Absalom wished he was alone with no responsibilities and no powers so he could enjoy a simple life with his family but I cut it out because I thought it would contradict his want to be a protector of the innocent.

A Union of Hearts:
Repairing the Familial Pillar
Albert Oon

*concept art of Absalom & his specters

Chapter 1 – A Second Chance Unwasted

I look at my family and treasure being with them every day of my life as if it is my last day, especially today since it may be my last. A force of conceited people has grown in the world and is imposing their false truth on those they conquer or deceive. Many allied kingdoms have willingly fallen to their lies, are in flames, or are enslaved by the conceited. There are even those in the Church of the Absolute who preach their falsehoods and started their own churches to convert more of the faithful, the ignorant, and the uninformed. The few kingdoms still dedicated to the truth like the kingdom I live in, Simbiosi, are attacked on all sides and the capital that I live in will soon be under attack.

Today, I am allowed to spend the beginning of the day with them before I join the troops out of the walls to help defend against a potential attack. Many times, I have lost my family, but the Absolute has blessed me with this new one. I cannot help but be in constant fear for their safety. If the conceited were to take them over my dead body, they would be enslaved or killed as they have done with many families.

"Are you worrying again, Absalom?" my wife Estella says while looking at me with concern on her face.

Since our hearts are connected, my wife can typically read me like a book. I sometimes wish she couldn't so she wouldn't be concerned by my useless worries and weaknesses.

"I must confess that I am. I'm sorry," I say before looking away in shame.

Estella leans over so I can see her comforting smile.

"It's going to be okay. I'll be singing for you and the troops to give you strength."

"Your singing has always been our key to victory along with yours, Mia."

My daughter, Mia, can also sing like her mother and even summon specters like I can except she can only summon two animals whereas I can summon up to fifteen spectral soldiers to aid me in battle.

"Is there something that I can do besides that?" Mia asks.

"You can pray as you sing," I suggest.

"I can help you in battle."

"No, you can't."

"Yes, I can! This is what my Heart Absolute ability was made for."

"You can use an elephant and a hawk for more than battle."

"What am I supposed to be then? A performer? A clown in the circus? I know what my heart's purpose is."

"I don't want you getting hurt or killed in battle."

"I won't get killed if I just use my specters. I'll use them to fight and bear whatever pain comes with it."

"How do you know you won't get killed? Your ability isn't like exactly like mine and it hasn't been tested yet."

"If I do get injured badly, then I'll leave and get medical help, I promise! Please, let me help defend our home, father."

"No, I will not. Not now at least."

Mia gives me a look of bitter resignation before looking down and away from me and then leaving the table.

"Mia."

"She's just like you," Estella points out.

"I honestly hope that she turns out more like you or at least takes the best of both of us while leaving out the worst."

I go outside where Mia is sitting on the porch.

"I know how you feel," I say.

"Then you'd let me help you fight," Mia says.

"When the time is right."

"I'm old enough to fight and have two powerful specters with me that I can summon anywhere I can think of like you."

"You just turned sixteen last month."

"That's old enough for the prince and princess's new children to start their training. Knowing them, they probably started their training earlier."

"You aren't like them. You're my daughter and the Absolute has a different role in life for you."

"I know that. I just feel that I found it."

"I thought that I found my true role in life when I recklessly followed my heart. People here still view me as a villain because of the death and destruction I caused because of it. I admit that I'm afraid of you getting hurt and even more afraid of you dying, but I'm most afraid of you making the same mistakes I made."

"I understand. I pray I could do something to change the minds of those who still view you in a negative light."

"They'll change their minds in time. For now, hone your ability and after the battle, we'll train your specters to see if they can fight. Maybe you can act as support for the troops such as using your hawk for scouting or using your elephant to break through the enemy's walls."

"Okay."

I hug Mia and she hugs me. Before we can go inside, a group of soldiers come to my door and let me know it's time to go. Turning to Estella and Mia, I promise them that I'll be back and then head out with the soldiers to meet the rest of the army outside of the walls. The soldiers take me to Prince Caleb and Princess Kyla who are at the frontlines of the capital's defense.

"Hello, Absalom. Is your daughter going to use her specters to aid us in battle?" Caleb asks.

"No, but she will be giving us strength with her singing just like her mother. Are your children going to be fighting with us?" I say.

"They'll fight if the fighting gets inside the walls. What's with that look on your face? I only asked because she told me that she wants to fight. What's the harm in letting her? She won't die if her specters are dissipated in battle like yours, right?"

"I don't know if she will or not."

"Caleb, he's afraid of his daughter getting hurt or dying," Kyla says.

"Given his record of dead wives and daughters, I understand."

"Caleb!"

"What? I'm just speaking bluntly and mean nothing by it. I'm sorry if what I said hurt you, Absalom. It's just that…I feel as uneasy as you do and want to use every resource I have to obtain victory for us."

"And you'd use my daughter?"

"No, I won't force her to fight like the enemy does. Forget I said anything. Anyways, this is our first time fighting together. Do you think you can fight as well as you did when you fought us? I've heard good things from the commanders you were under."

I'd prefer it if Caleb also forgot when he and Kyla brought me to justice. Leave the past in the past. I've already served my penance for my sins and need to look forward to the future.

"Just wait and see. Has your downtime weakened your skills?"

"Parenting has done that a bit, but Kyla and I have been sparring to keep in shape. We're also competing to see who wins the most sparing match. I'm winning by the way."

"Not if you're counting my victories," Kyla says.

"You mean the ones I let you have?"

"You always say that as an excuse for the times I beat you."

"It's the truth, not an excuse."

Despite Caleb's manners, he's still a good prince of justice. Kyla is also an amazing princess of mercy. Both are faithful servants of the Absolute who is the king of this kingdom and the guide of our hearts. Even though I'd like to forget the times when I wasn't myself, I am thankful for them and the Absolute for bringing me back to my senses whenever I remember my shameful failings. Kyla and Caleb will be flying around the battlefield where they are needed while I and the other soldiers will defend other parts of the outer walls.

Soon after I take my defensive position, the enemy goes pouring in. We heard they were coming and rushed to get ready. Caleb and Kyla didn't have enough time to do their battle speech to raise morale, but at least we made it on time. I spawn fifteen specters with a variety of weapons to aid me and my fellow soldiers in battle while they use their variety of Heart Absolute abilities as well. The conceited use their abilities as well, but since their abilities are inversions of their own or weaker versions of others, we have the advantage in terms of power. For example, one of them that I face that lights himself on fire and can manifest weapons is defeated by my simple sword and shield whereas one of my fellow soldiers who can use similar fire powers can take on multiple foes without being hit. It also helps that I can feel strengthened by Estella's and Mia's singing which gives me the strength I need to endure the hits that my specters take.

Kyla and Caleb eventually fly over us and use their dragons of mercy and justice to spray their flames upon our enemies. The ones who still have some good in their soul are simply knocked out by the flames while the ones who are judged to be damned are burned to ash. These flames are the manifestation of the Absolute's judgment and seeing them reminds me of when I was purified of the temptations in my head by those blessed flames. I, along with the rest of the soldiers, cheer for them as they fly by. Wait. What's that near Caleb? Is that a white hawk with grey wings? Sending up one of my specters to check, I find that my eyes do not deceive me. It's my daughter's hawk specter who is telling Caleb where to go.

Through my specter, I catch my daughter's hawk by the wings before she can escape me and then say, "What do you think you're doing, Mia?!"

"I'm doing what I'm called to, father," she says.

"Don't worry about her, Absalom. We'll take care of her," Caleb says.

"But-"

"It's a promise and an order for you to leave her in our protection."

"Fine. Be careful, Mia."

With nothing more to say or do, I focus on the battle and try to end it on my side so that it ends quicker and any threat to Mia is erased. Eventually, the conceited retreat. We think victory is ours until a rumbling in the ground puts us on our guard until a giant black and white dragon with five heads that seems to be half as large as the capital appears in front of us in an explosion of fire. Caleb, Kyla, and I along with the other soldiers focus on this creature and attack it with everything we have. The conceited that retreated moments ago come back in full force to defend the dragon as it charges forward to the capital. It's about to charge through the walls until Mia's elephant appears which is about the size of a castle's wall and stops it by charging into it. This allows the wall's defenders and we keep the dragon in place as we cut at its legs to cripple it.

"Our hearts and strength become one and closer than they ever have before," Caleb and Kyla say in one voice, "Face the judgment of a pure heart!"

Caleb and Kyla's dragon becomes a singular dragon that they ride on. This dragon called the Judgment of the Absolute breathes its gold and black fire on the multiheaded dragon while flying around it until the dragon burns to ash and the only thing left of it is a single conceited man with many heads on his body. What they just did is something that I wish to try with my own family since people who love each other and have Heart Absolute abilities can combine their abilities into a powerful singular ability they both control with one heart and mind. I along with Caleb, Kyla, and the other troops surround this man ready to bring him in for questioning.

"This isn't over. You're going to wish that you lost this battle," the man says.

"What are you talking about? You're the one who has lost," Caleb says.

"Heh, I'll give you a hint. You don't think that everyone in your kingdom is loyal to you, do you? We were going to take the capital with as much minimal damage as possible, but you leave us no choice. You'll have ruins for homes."

After the man says this, he dies and then multiple explosions happen throughout the capital. From where we are, we can see the largest buildings collapse and be blown up from the inside. If that's not enough, a dark fog emerges in the capital as we rush in. Screams and sounds of fighting echo from every corner of the capital that forces the army to disperse to quell the chaos. At a time like this, I wish Mia would disobey my order so she could tell me where she and her mother are and what's happening.

I send out my specters in haste to help every citizen I can and send out two extra ones to find my family. Making these two extra ones takes more strength, but thankfully, I can still feel the effects of Estella's and Mia's singing, so they must be alive. As I rush back home, I see people disappearing into the dark through my specters. My specters try to save these people, but those that disappear are gone without a trace which means that whatever is in the dark fog teleports its victims to a different place. We'll have to find these people later. Meanwhile, the only threats I can deal with are the conceited that are trying to kill whoever they can.

Have mercy on us all, Absolute. Do not let the conceited take our families from us and make the conceited see the error of their ways. Keep everyone safe and give us the strength to get through these challenging times.

"Father!" I hear the sound of Mia and the sons and daughters of Caleb and Kyla say.

My specters catch their cries and do what they can to save them from the many conceited that are targeting them. To combat the growing number of enemies, I summon more specters so that I have a total of twenty out with ten protecting my family and ten protecting Caleb and Kyla's children. Mia uses her elephant to help defend her mother and Caleb and Kyla's children don't have much of a problem defending themselves. Still, I have to take some of the hits for them by making my specters block the enemies' attacks with their bodies. The pain slows me down a bit, but my determination and offering up the pain as penance keep me going until I finally get to where my family is.

"Estella! Mia!" I yell out to them.

They call back out to me before Estella and Mia continue their singing. I'm comforted at the sight of their safety, but even more on edge to keep them safe, especially since it seems like the conceited are countless and endlessly come out of the dark fog.

Turning to Mia and Estella, I say, "We should combine our Heart Absolute abilities together to push them back!"

"I've never done it before," Mia says.

"What would mine do to help? I think it'd be best if I kept singing," Estella says.

"Look at me and don't worry. Grab my hands and join your hearts with mine. The Absolute will take care of the rest."

Mia and Estella look at me and then do as I told them.

With one voice we say, "Three turns into one as the three are one in the Absolute. One family, one heart, and one Absolute."

A light bursts out from us. From it comes hundreds of soldiers on unicorns, elephants, and griffins all clothed in a bright white light that dispels the darkness and overwhelms the conceited. The soldiers and their animals sing to everyone in the capital to lift their spirits and strengthen them while also demoralizing the enemy and piercing their ears with our songs. Together, we drive them off along with the dark fog. Victory is finally ours despite the many lives lost and the destruction done to our homes.

We combined our hearts and used a powerful ability just like the prince and princess. Father, that was amazing! It was and so were you, Mia and Estella. The Absolute saved us in our time of need and I came back as promised. This is all great and I don't mean to spoil the mood, but can we stop using this power of ours, Absalom? Using it for this long makes me feel like I've been running for hours.

Oh, of course, Estella. I'm sorry, mother. I didn't notice the strain it put on you. Show offs. Acting like it was nothing.

Estella was right. It feels like a heavy weight is taken off my shoulders now that we've stopped using our combined hearts' ability. Anyways, I'm glad that we're all safe now. Even though the capital is in ruins and we've lost many, I'm confident that this isn't the end for us and we'll come back stronger and ready to fight again.

*concept art of Estella

Chapter 2 – The Cross of Being Supportive

"Are you okay, Estella?" Absalom asks me.

It takes a moment for me to respond as I look back upon the ruins of the capital and our home.

"Yes, I'm fine," I say.

He gives a reassuring smile and nod before looking forward and keeping his eyes open for any threats on the road. Right now, I'm sitting on a horse-drawn wagon with other people as everyone in the capital leaves it along with everything necessary we need. After so many attacks, our capital and home are nothing but ruins and wreckage. The prince and princess have talked to a nearby city so that we can live in it for the time being until our enemies are defeated and homes rebuilt. It'll take a while to get there. I wish we could have a person who could teleport us to the next city, but apparently, all the people who can do it are busy helping other kingdoms and people around the world who are in similar situations to us.

This is not to say that I don't trust the protection of the prince and princess and our army as we make this long and dangerous trip. I just feel worried about the safety of everyone who can't defend themselves and most of all, I feel useless. Even my daughter, Mia, can defend herself and others and is now part of the force defending the carts thanks to proving herself in the recent battles. She stands proud with her father and is attentive just like him. My singing has helped them though, which they say was integral in us surviving the enemy's attacks. Of this, I have no doubt. Through my ability, I can feel the hearts of those that my singing affects rise in strength.

The princess and those who act as support for others have the ability to feel the hearts of others, and others, such as the princess, can even tell the destination of a heart to see if it goes to the heavenly Land of the True or the hellish Land of the Forgotten. My Heart Absolute ability isn't as grand as hers and is much simpler. I try to treasure it and believe that my singing does do good, but the temptation to doubt its helpfulness is always there. There was hardly a use for my singing before I met Absalom. I sang for those that I prayed for, the weak, the dying, and the soldiers fighting for our kingdom. After we met, the power of my singing increased and I felt as if my life's purpose was found. Still, I don't feel completely satisfied.

Perhaps it's why the Absolute brought Absalom and me together. Both of us want to do more for the people we love and feel like we can never do enough. Mia shares

much of the same feeling as a result. It's a blessed curse as

some say so that we remember to always rely on the

Absolute and that we can never truly do enough for those

we love. Instead, we must always do something for them no

matter how small. These things are what I believe, know to

be true, and what I keep telling myself to stay positive and

not sulk in my own weakness. Despite me fighting these

temptations, how I feel still shows on my face and it seems

like Absalom and Mia have noticed as they look at me and

whisper to themselves.

"Why don't you sing and lift everyone's spirits,

Estella?" Absalom suggests.

"Yeah, show them what you can do!" Mia cheers

me on.

Looking at the people in my cart, a couple of them

are attentive waiting for me to sing while a few others seem

disgusted. There are some in the kingdom who still distrust

Absalom because of his past and even call me and Mia cursed to die a horrible death because of what happened to his first three wives and children. Nervous, I look back to Absalom and Mia who smile and nod at me. Well, if anything happens, I'll at least have them to protect me. As I start to sing, I can feel the hearts of those that I sing for.

Many are stressed and many more are on the edge of despair. I am thankful that there are those including my family and the prince and princess appreciate what I can do while trying not to be offended by those that don't want the comfort of my singing. In terms of my songs, I haven't created any original poems, songs, or melodies of my own nor do I sing songs with lyrics since I find it difficult to remember all the lyrics exactly and when I mess up, I mess up the effectiveness of my singing. Because of this, I sing melodies without any actual lyrics. Eventually, some who have hardened hearts relax and the air around us seems to slowly be relieved of the tension in it. That is until one of the people I'm singing for is disturbed by some people approaching us, which stops me from singing.

From where I am, I see a group of cloaked wanderers approaching us with many bags on their backs and hands. They seem like the homeless I've seen before who entered our capital seeking our home because of the conceited, however, they start to change when they are in the middle of our group. Many people come out of each person as if the person had portals to other places in almost every part of their body. In addition, the trees around us transform into groups of people all of which attack us. Soon after the same accursed dark fog that's been kidnapping people falls over us as Absalom, Mia, and the other defenders try to fight off the attack. Despite their best efforts, the fog grows thicker and thicker until everything around me is darkness and I can't even see my hands in front of my face.

The darkness eventually lifts and the noise of fighting subsides. I'm comforted for a second before realizing that I've been teleported somewhere completely different away from where I was, and I must be far away because I don't hear anything around me not even the sounds of the ambush I was in.

"Absalom! Mia!" I call out.

For some reason, I think they'll hear me. It's useless. There's no choice for me but to wander through the woods to find my way back to my family. The hearts of family are connected by an invisible thread that not many know how to use. I have some experience with being able to use these threads especially since I'm able to touch the hearts of people. There was one time I found Mia when wandered off to fight some kids who badmouthed her father and bullied her friends. Absalom scolded her for defending him but not so much for defending her friends.

Remembering what it felt like to follow the thread, I use the faint feeling of it to find my way back to my family.

It's not long after wandering do I hear the noises of someone else in the forest with me. Unsure of who it is, I hide behind one of the trees to see who it is. A woman dressed in shadows glides through the shadows looking in every direction. She looks to be conceited because of the hole I can see in her chest and her grey and black eyes.

"Come out, wife of Absalom, and I will make sure that your family receives a place of honor in our kingdom. In fact, your family may be all we need to win this battle against the Absolute," the woman says.

She knows who I am. It's no wonder why I got teleported out here.

"I know you're around here," she continues, "The shadows are my domain. Even if you get far, I'll bring my fog upon you and bring you back to me. Make this easier for both of us. I have a family of my own to take care of."

That doesn't make what you're doing justified in any way. Right now, I'm slowly trying to get away from her even as she teleports from shadow to shadow in an instant.

"If that's how you're going to be, then so be it."

The dark fog spreads from the woman's mouth and covers everything around me in darkness. I can't see and I'm defenseless without my family. My Heart Absolute can't help me here…unless…maybe if I can touch her heart and convince her to stop. Since I have no other choice, I take this option and start singing and focus on touching her heart rather than amplifying her strength.

"What is this? What are you doing? Is this your way of saying that you surrender?"

"No, it isn't. I feel your pain and your fear," I say while I am able to sing at the same time.

"I'm not afraid of you."

"But what are you afraid of? Will something happen to your family if you don't take my family?"

"That's none of your business."

"But you did mention that you have a family to take care of. What will happen to them if you fail? Perhaps my kingdom can free them."

"Your kingdom and God can do nothing. It's more complex than just my kingdom and its allies."

"Through the Absolute, all is possible such as me knowing the truth within your heart. You want to believe that we can help so let us."

The woman appears right in front of my face and almost stops me from singing.

"You're nothing compared to them, my masters that have enslaved and slaughtered many. You do not know their strength or their cruelty."

"I can know it through your heart. I sense the fear for your children and husband. They're in…much pain."

"How do you know that?!"

"Because your heart is connected to theirs. What's happening to them?"

"Why do you care?!"

"Because I care about the suffering of others, unlike your masters. You can tell me what's happening to them and we'll help. Feel the honesty and conviction in my heart."

"…what you're feeling is just a taste of the suffering I know. The men work twelve hours a day with little time to breathe in between. Children are indoctrinated and work much like the adults and are punished like adults if they resist. Women are prevented from having too many children or are used as breeding stock to have more. Everyone is punished severely for mistakes or rebellion and their punishments such as being forced to starve to death in public make them wish for the death penalty. All are subject to the desires and will of the masters. All are disposable and can be used for whatever reasons they have. If I didn't take this role in the army, my family would've been forced to work harder or be punished for my actions."

The pain from her heart causes me to recoil a bit, however, I don't let go and embrace the pain instead to relieve her of it. This relief shows on her face as some of the anger on it disappears.

"We'll save them and help you. Trust me."

The woman's pained heart slowly breaks under the pressure of my honesty. Part of her heart is filled, color is restored to her skin, and her eyes become blue and white.

"Please...save them. Help us," she says as she tries not to cry.

"We will. Can you get me back to my family?"

"Yes, of course."

After the woman's dark fog comes over us, we appear not too far from Absalom and Mia.

"Absalom! Mia!" I call out to them while running to them.

They see and call out to me and run to meet and hug me. I almost cry from my happiness to see that they're still alive.

"I'm so glad that you've found your way to us," Absalom says until he sees the woman behind me. He then holds me and Mia in closer probably because she still looks conceited. "Who is she?"

"Don't worry about her. She helped me find you and is no longer as conceited as she seems. I've convinced her that we'll save her family."

"We can do that, but first we must regroup with the prince, princess, and the others."

"We can try, but it'll be difficult, especially with the prince and princess whom I put somewhere dangerous," the woman says.

"You what?"

"She controls the dark fog that has been teleporting us around because her masters forced her to with her family's lives on the line," I say.

"I see. Well, I can relate to that motive. What's your name?"

"Leilani."

"Leilani, we'll help rescue your family. First, let's see how many people we can reunite with so we can better do that, okay?"

"Okay."

Leilani tries to help us find people from our kingdom, however, we're only able to find a few with the fate of the others up in the air while some have tragically died. While looking for the prince and princess where Leilani teleported them, we find the place in ruins with the ashes and knocked out conceited around the area so it's safe to say that they survived and left the area.

"I'm sorry we could hardly find anyone and I'm especially sorry for the ones that died," Leilani says with her head down.

"Don't worry about it. With all our abilities combined, I think we have enough people to free your family," Absalom says.

"Do you really think so? The place where my family is isn't exactly a city, but it is heavily guarded and even its citizens will be forced to fight with the threat of severe humiliating punishment looming over them if they don't. Not everyone who will fight you wants to. You must be careful with these people."

"We'll do our best," I say.

"We will and we'll save your family, many of the innocent, and bring your masters to justice," Absalom adds.

"Yeah! We promise!" Mia also adds.

Our fellow citizens that we found cheer and bring a smile to Leilani's face.

She tries not to cry as she says, "Thank you, everyone."

"Now, bring us to them, but not too close," Absalom says, "We don't want to immediately alert them to our attack."

"Okay!"

Leilani's dark fog comes over us. Absolute, grant us the strength and skill we need to save not only her family, but the many families that need our help, and thank you for letting my ability grow so that I know it's not as meager as I once thought it was.

*concept art of Mia and her specters

Chapter 3 – Worthy Successor and the Power of Familial Love

Inaction always makes me anxious and knowing that injustice is happening to the innocent with nothing being done to save them makes me even more anxious.

"Stop moving around, Mia. We must be patient," my father, Absalom, whispers.

I do as he asks. He seems to be feeling the same way as I see him subtlety fidget a bit every now and then, especially when he sees some injustice happening such as people being worked to death or cruelly beaten and being chained to a spot as a live example to the others. The hearts of a family are connected and I know for certain that he and my mother feel the same way I do. For the past five or so hours, we've been scouting out this town that's been remade into a city and trying to free as many people as we can before we attack its leaders. My father uses his specters to direct our smaller groups of allies while I use two hawks for surveillance to help them know what's ahead of them.

We're making progress, but there are hundreds of people here and someone will eventually notice that some are missing. Speaking of that, some of the more attentive guards have noticed this. Most of these guards we knocked out while converting some to our side with Leilani's help. I'm still amazed that mother was able to convert her. I don't know why I am though. My mother has always been able to change and uplift hearts with her singing and kind words. What I'm more confused about is when she feels sad about not being able to do anything when she goes above and beyond not only for her family but for others as well with her singing.

Perhaps this worry of not doing enough runs in the family and why the Absolute brought my mother and father together since they share the problem and need to get over it together. Eventually, the number of missing people becomes clear to too many guards to silence or convert and the alarm is raised forcing us to shift to the second part of our plan. Since I'm able to spawn specters where I've been or places I've seen and I've been and have seen most places in this city, I summon elephants that appear in certain places to cause chaos to break watch towers and injury as many guards and soldiers as I can. Along with my father's specters, we make our forces seem bigger than they are by appearing and reappearing in many places causing lots of damage as we can while evacuating everyone that we can.

War, Love, and the Absolute

My mother and I sing to strengthen the hearts of the converted and allies though she tries to convert the hearts of our enemies by mostly by herself since I hardly know what to do. Still, she gets me to help her with this and say what I can to change hearts and aid them. The battle is going our way. I'm especially thankful for Leilani who teleports people to safety with her dark fog that also acts as a cover. We look like we're going to win until we start hearing reports of people dropping dead in our area and reinforcements for the enemy's arrival.

I black out for a second then come to my senses seemingly minutes later with my parents trying to get me up. They look like they're trying not to cry, but they're happy and hugging me now that I've woken up from whatever came over me. For some reason, we're in a dark room that's like a large prison cell with many people on the floor above us looking down at us as if we were animals in a zoo.

"What happened?" I ask.

"I'll answer that for you," a man cloaked in the dark says. "After all the chaos you caused, we decided to take matters into our own hands and take you ourselves. Because of your reputation, Absalom, we'll give you the honor of giving you our names. Mine is Nixon. My fellow negotiators are Griffen who can bring you back to life and heal your wounds by breathing on you and Pasito who made you black out or rather put you in a near death state just by looking at you. Be thankful to your God that I find you useful. Otherwise, I'd have you feel the pain of the worse deaths possible. Speaking of that, you will experience some of the worse deaths possible if you do not agree to ally with us."

"Do you really think-"

"Ab-"

Before I can blink, both of my parents drop to the ground. Their eyes are red and their mouths are frothing.

"Mother…father…" I say quivering and unable to move to check on them.

"Don't worry about them. We'll bring them back to life in just a second."

Nixon snaps his fingers and Griffen blows his breath from the floor above us and brings father and mother gasping, crying, and screaming back to life. They try to stop to compose themselves, put a lid on their reactions, and hide their faces from me.

"Did you like that way of dying? Death by over a thousand cuts. It's the one I have Pasito use first since it gets people on my side the quickest. I'll have you know that Pasito can induce many forms of pain in you because he's witnessed and felt the worst. So, what's your answer now?" Nixon says.

"…we…that's not going to be enough to stop us," my father answers.

"We…won't give in!" my mother adds.

My father then tries using one of his specters to attack the people above us, but then mother-I-I. I feel like I'm being eaten alive! Get these bugs off me! Get them out of me!

"Mia! Mia!" my father says while holding my shaking body.

I hold him and cry in his arms unable to cope with what just happened to me.

"Death by being eaten alive by special kinds of bugs. Horrifying to see which is why a person is buried alive in addition to being killed that way. How did it feel Absalom?" Nixon says.

My father doesn't bother to look at him and instead tries to hold in his anger as he tries to think of something to do.

"You're horrible people!" my mother says.

"We are, I admit, but it's for a very good reason, and hopefully this can help convince you to ally with us.

You already knew this reason, Absalom. You fell far from the glory that we aspire to. We were going to have you join us, but you changed before we had all our forces organized."

"Spit it out already. Why are you doing this?" my father asks.

"To replace an aging truth. Face it, Absalom. The Church and her kingdoms are a relic of the past and may have once been invincible, but it is no longer as you have seen with its dwindling territories. Your God has abandoned you and is no longer the truth. Our truth is better anyway. People are freer and happier than they were before. I know you've seen the ugly side of it, but it's a necessary evil so that people in the future will enjoy the works of today."

"You enslave and kill those that disagree."

"Haven't you?"

"I kill only when I'm forced to."

"We do the same. As far as I'm concerned, killing is always done in self-defense. You're either defending yourself physically or defending whatever god, love, or truth has hold of our hearts. I think even your prince admitted to the fact that we live in a world that's always filled with war."

"You don't understand anything," my mother says.

"What don't I understand?"

"You don't understand reality, love, truth, or the Absolute, which is love and truth itself-"

My mother drops to the ground.

"Don't try using your ability. Pasito can feel hearts and know when you are using it."

I black out soon after and feel like my entire body is on fire. Waking up again, I can't help but cry and puke.

"You're lucky that I have enough respect for you that I told Pasito not to let you imagine dying by having you defecate yourself," Nixon says as he begins to sound impatient.

"You won't get away with this," my father says.

"Says who? Think about it one last time. Absolute freedom. That's what I'm fighting for. Being free from the Absolute, defining yourself, and doing what you want to do with your life is the definition of absolute freedom rather than being a slave to a truth or what you call love."

"I'd rather be a slave to truth and love than to be a slave to your false truth," I manage to say while holding back my tears.

"Our daughter is right," my father and mother say.

I think for a second that we're going to combine our hearts together to use a combined ability, however, we aren't able to. We continuously die over and over again while feeling the worst ways to die. Nixon keeps telling us to join him in different ways and single sentences as to why his freedom is the right way. My father, mother, and I keep denying him and keep dying. Is this it? Are we going to keep suffering like this until we break and give in? Has the Absolute abandoned us to this? Maybe if we give in, we can find a way out after?

Don't think that way, Mia. Father? There's another way to overcome them. Violence isn't always the answer. Do you remember what the truest act of love is? To suffer for another? Yes, that's it. Unite your heart with ours and offer up your suffering to the Absolute as penance for our sins, the sins of the faithful, and the sins of the people that oppress us. Mother, I don't think I can do it for them. I feel so much hatred for the people doing this to us. It's okay, Mia. I feel it too, but love is more than a feeling. It's action. That's right.

Continuously, we keep dying, however, in the suffering, I can feel peace. Pain keeps trying to drag me away from it, but I persist with the help of my parents. I understand now. We understand. We've always known.

The Absolute has already shown us by His example. Even in the midst of defeat and the darkest times, truth and love will always exist and prevail. Our victories are His. Our failures are ours. We let go of our worries and embrace this truth. We embrace the suffering of one another and love those who hate us for this is real truth and love.

"Please, get up," one of Nixon's men says to us.

It's Griffen who is helping us up. People around us are fighting and on the floor near us is Nixon who appears to have died a death by defecation. Next to Griffen is Pasito who is making others that he looks at drop dead.

"We're sorry," Griffen says.

"Wha-what happened?" I ask with my head spinning from all the pain.

"The love gushing forth from your hearts touched everyone in the room. We were hearing…whispers. Voices telling us to stop and reasons for doing so. The reason that surprised us the most was that you were suffering for us. Is this true?"

"We were," my father says.

"Why? It doesn't make sense for you to," Pasito says.

"It does if you know what it means to truly love," my mother says.

"I think I know what you mean even though I can hardly begin to explain it," Griffen says.

"The answer still puzzles me," Pasito says.

"But you know it otherwise you wouldn't have acted the way you did."

"I did it because the voices compelled me to and I didn't want to be a slave to Nixon and the other masters anymore."

"We'll find the answer together later. First, we must get out of here."

"We should bring Nixon and the others with us and they should be alive," my father says.

"Why should we do that to those scum?" Pasito says.

"Because I was once scum and now, I am a real man. Give them a second chance even though they don't seem to deserve it. That is part of what true love is."

Pasito and Griffen look at each other before Griffen shrugs his shoulders and agrees, but first, we secure the facility we are in, tie up Nixon, and his supporters before bringing them back to life.

"What…how am I…Why did you?" Nixon asks.

"The Absolute will answer those questions for you in due time," my father says.

We ascend from the facility to the surface to see that we were in some kind of castle with a large underground portion to it. When we exit it, we're surprised to find the prince and princess with an army behind them breaking through the gates.

The prince approaches us and says to my father, "You really had to steal all the glory? What are you doing here? How did you capture the enemy leaders?"

My father wraps his arms around my mother and me and then says, "My family was the key to victory."

"That's obvious. Explain everything to me."

"That's going to take a while."

"Of course. Soldiers, take the prisoners away. Absalom, we have a long journey to our new home so you'll have plenty of time to tell me the whole story."

"Yes, sir."

Even though this ended in a way that I didn't expect and I'm sure that we'll have more enemies to face later, I'm glad that it's over. The enemy disregarded the Absolute and the family that are the cause of their defeat and main supports of society and hearts, and now suffer the consequences for it. I'm glad for everything that my father and mother have done for me because we would be lost without the truth and love that they taught and showed me through their example. They showed me that through true love for each other and with all our hearts combined as one family, anything is possible and that nothing can overcome true love.

The End

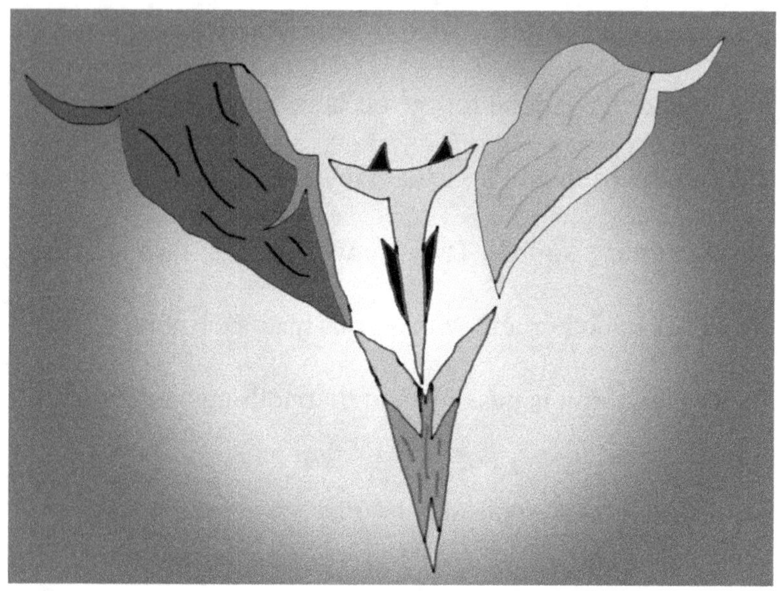

Concept art for the heart of the family.

War, Love, and the Absolute

- Originally, the story was meant to just be about Estella and Mia finding their way to Absalom after their home was destroyed with Absalom's specters helping them get to him and them witnessing how the family is being exploited, but I thought this family story would be better if they were together.

- I didn't mention it, but both Estella and Mia are wearing armor under their clothes and Estella is wear a veil made of chainmail kind of like Absalom's parents.

- The heart of the family looks similar to the heart of the Absolute since God is where all authority, especially the authority of the father and mother come from.

If you liked these stories, then check out these other ones!

What will you sacrifice for your child? Both of these dark fantasy short stories filled with songs/poems are about a parent who is trying to save the life of their dying child. A father must travel a desert wasteland infested with fiends and their slaves to get the cure for his daughter at the top of the world. A mother journeys across a beautiful crystal world that is at war with itself to help her shattering son. Both of these parents will risk their lives in order to ensure that their children will live on, but can they when they have everything in the world against them?

Cinis and Favilla are a couple trained to be the hope for the Kingdom of Fornax. Humanity fights against the forces of rot and decay with fire and light so that they can continue living, but these are uncertain times. "The greatest act of all is love," is the saying that Fornax goes by. Will the love between Cinis and Favilla be enough to hold them together through their challenges or will they eventually rot away like the rest of the world? Love burns brighter than fire in this fantasy tale with grand action scenes and moments to remember.

Are you as good a person as you think you are? These three stories are all about the choices we make and the consequences they reap. A young boy gains ten million dollars at the cost of his family, friends, and normal life. A teenage girl stresses herself to become famous at the cost of having terrible nightmares. A man runs away from his guilts and finds himself in a town that punishes the guilty that evade earthly justice. Will these people live with their choices or die because of their consequences?

Love is the Ultimate Weapon Against Sin In these three short stories, love finds a way to overcome evil. Love burns away the sins of the past. Love ends wars and destroys hatred. Love is more valuable than anything in the world and can change it. Find out how love does this in this collection where love is the ultimate weapon against evil.

Check out these free eBooks on Smashwords as well!

Not many people want to admit when they're wrong, but Zayden realizes his mistakes after a prank almost costs him the life of his friend, he promises to change. He wants to repent but demons put him in a supernatural trap with three people close to him that they've turned into monsters. He must now save these people that he's hurt if he wants to save himself.

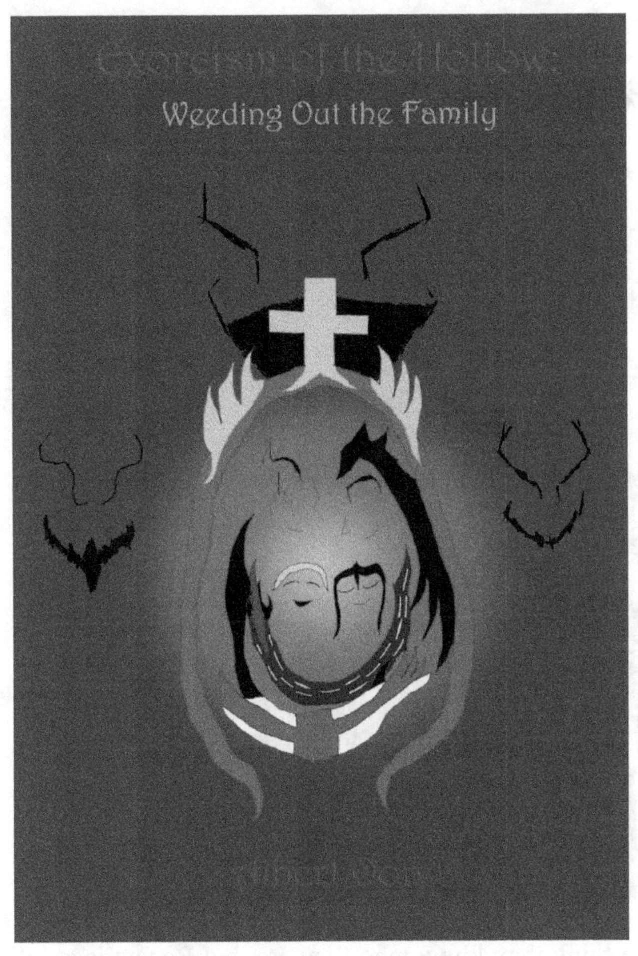

While bickering with his father-in-law, Triton, Alessio is surprised to find that the home of the exorcists is under attack by demons and hollows who claim to be from his mother's side of the family. These hollows kidnap his children and are stern in their devotion to sin. Now, Alessio must fight the difficult battle of fighting his family who would rather go to Hell than Heaven.

How to Build Yourself

Albert Oon

Many people think they know who they are, but Renata is a doll that wants to find out who exactly she is and why she should care about what she does in life. She'll travel through the doll factory that she lives in and interact with many people to learn why they live the way they do with some dolls being more strange and dangerous than others.

A king has died fighting tyranny and giving his life for those he loved and his son, Bane, takes his place. In this land where kingdoms are founded on various fields of knowledge, Bane will try to make allies in this new world free of tyranny and understand each kingdom, even the kingdom where his father's killer was from. This book is created by Nikolay Panev and written by Albert Oon.

Albert Oon

Check out my blog, Albert Oon: Behind the Stories, for free

short stories, free book samples, song/poem attempts, and more!

Follow me on Twitter, Facebook, Instagram, and LinkedIn to see

what I'm doing next.